Misadventures of Wunderwear Woman Down Under

Denis Hayes

PARTRIDGE

A Penguin Random House Company

To order additional copies of this book, contact
Toll Free 800 101 2657 (Singapore)
Toll Free 1 800 81 7340 (Malaysia)
orders.singapore@partridgepublishing.com

www.partridgepublishing.com/singapore

Other books by the same author :-

Children's books, Website :- www.sillystorycentre.com

Silly Animal Stories for Kids
Silly Fishy Stories for Kids
Silly Ghost Stories for Kids

Teen books, Website :- www.sillystorycentre.com

Silly Alien Space Stories for Bigger Kids
Silly Alien Space War Stories for Bigger Kids
Silly Alien Space Time Travel Stories for even Bigger Kids
Out of this World Stories

Adult Books, Website :- www.theoffensivebookcentre.com

The Misadventures of Wunderwear Woman
The Misadventures of Wunderwear Woman in America
Bye Bye Baby Boy Big Boy Blues
Hard Travellin' Man Blues

Denis Hayes -
Author & Illustrator

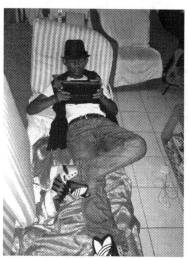

Danish Aikal Hayes -
Cover Creator

Lance and Isabel, still happy, still married, still solid. Wunderwear Woman is the third party in their lives. Isabel releases her only on special occasions!

She had started her Wunderwear Woman crusade because she wanted to change the world but found that the world had changed her. She hoped not too much but some said not nearly enough. Even so she was still more than a handful.

The Wedding

Isabel was no longer the woman she used to be - Wunderwear Woman! She used to be huge and magnificent. She was still magnificent, after all she was a woman, but she was no longer huge. Hard work and a strenuous sex life had reduced surplus body weight to containable levels. She was amazed and happy.

Married life agreed with her. Her husband Lance was great.

However she still punched well above her reduced weight whenever she was faced with injustice and bullshit.

She was in fact still Wunderwear Woman inside. It was merely a superficial cosmetic change on the outside.

For the time being the family buzz was not about her. It was all about The Wedding. The wedding of her sister in law Jeanette to Russ, the youthful bushwacking style Australian who had swept her off her feet in the best romantic novel Barbara Cartland style.

He was coming over to the USA with family and friends so that they could marry in Florida and then go back together and settle in Australia.

Mom was fussing and flapping over the arrangements.

"Isabel," she said, "get the family together and make sure we have whisky and brandy on hand."

"Mom, what are you up to?" asked Isabel, "whenever we get extra licquor in it means we are in for a spot of religion. The Catholic religion, Irish style. What is going on?"

"Nothing, nothing at all," said Mom playing the innocent, "people are interested in the wedding is all."

"Yeah, what people?" chuckled Isabel, "Bishop Clancy and Father O'Halloran, am I right?"

"So, they married Jeanette first time out and confirmed all three of my bambinos at an early age. Of course they're interested," Mom said smugly, "pity you weren't catholic or they could have married you and Lance instead of that heathen Las Vegas Hollywood showman."

"Come on Ma you loved it, especially when he asked you if you were the bride's sister. For God's sake you fell for it, you actually fell for it, and came over all 'oh shucks you don't mean it' sort of thing, pulling your neckline down and twisting your bouquet into a knot. I thought you were never going to uncross your legs again."

"Never mind my legs, it was still a barbarian's wedding," Mom snorted, "anyways I wondered where God came in. I didn't hear him. The Reverend Fathers would have made sure he was there."

"Oh yeah, Father O'Halloran wouldn't have been asking for Jesus, he would have just asked for a refill and Clancy wouldn't have bothered to even do that. He would have just lifted up his empty glass."

"At least we got glasses, there wasn't one in sight when you got married. Bottles everywhere, no one waiting for a little refinement, and the way you and Lance danced I thought you'd get arrested," Mom complained.

"Brad did, remember," laughed Isabel, "with that lap dancer who couldn't get off after she got on. She wriggled down and got a shock because Brad expertly wriggled up. It wouldn't have been so obvious if she hadn't bent forwards to get away. They crawled across the floor doggie fashion, with Brad pushing forward and panting and the girl pushing backwards and moaning. Might not have been so bad if they hadn't crashed through the side doors into a Daughters of the Revolution meeting. Seems sex wasn't on their agenda that night, along with most other nights," Isabel reminisced, "anyway the officer's were pretty lenient. Put the two of them in the same cell to work it off."

"Oh yes, absolutely wonderful I don't think. It was disgraceful, Brad didn't want to be released," mused Mom, "the only one to refuse bail in years."

"I don't know about that," said Isabel, "I remember you saying that your sister Vera's husband turned up one night begging to be imprisoned and even paid the officers to refuse bail. He didn't want Vera to get anywhere near him. He was terrified."

"Serves him right, she wanted sex and he refused. Said he would rather hump a male hippo," said Mom firmly, "not a wise thing to say to Vera. With a gay son she's a bit touchy on the subject. She didn't mind the hippo but she hated it that he preferred a male. Disgusting. Took that personal!"

"When were you expecting the Fathers?" Isabel asked.

"Anytime they were free," answered Mom, "why?"

"Because they're here now. Holy Moses it's either in a taxi or a new car with a driver."

"What are you talking about?" Mom asked petulantly, "speak English."

"I thought I was," chuckled Isabel, "It's the Holy Fathers. They're here and they have a brand new Ford. You know - one of those that drives itself."

"Damn good job too because it might just stop O'Halloran from killing someone," exclaimed Mom, "let the family know and tell Brad to get the bottles in."

"Will do Mom."

Jeanette had made it to the door and ushered the two men into the room.

They all embraced.

"Wonderful isn't it Maria that the Christian religion is the only one you can really embrace. We not only embrace the religion but can embrace each other. If you embrace any other religion that's as far as it goes. Do it to any one else and you get arrested or stoned or something," chortled the Bishop, "most unhealthy."

"Stoned is it?" asked the Very Reverend Father O'Halloran, "isn't that illegal still. We haven't gone all liberal European over drugs now have we?"

"Not drugs Father," explained Isabel, "stones, like in bricks or rocks or whatever happens to be handy. Gentle Jesus said 'let he who is truly free from sin cast the first stone' but they're not bright enough to get that bit."

"My God, that's awful," O'Halloran cried, "we don't even allow our children to do that. You mean they encourage adults to do it?"

"Not just encourage Father," said Isabel, "they insist on it. They call it culture, tradition or justice as an excuse."

"They can call it what they like, stick any name on it, but they can't say it's civilised." O'Halloran wailed, "imagine you can hate, abuse and execute men and women in public but you can't give them a loving hug or a kiss. It's barbaric."

"Just like your driving Father," said the Bishop, "you may have noticed the new car Maria. Well we have a driver. We thought it safer. We don't want population control by Ford Motor Car to hit the headlines in Miami. The good Father saw the adverts and thought the car could really drive itself. He sat in it, started up, moved off and then read the newspaper. Fortunately the sales demonstrator gained control and stopped the car just before hitting a wall and collapsing with a panic attack."

"O'Halloran also had a bottle of fine Irish Whisky with him as he thought he could drink as he wasn't driving. The car was!! I worry sometimes as to what he says at Church Services let alone turning him loose at confessionals."

"Never mind Bishop, no one listens anyway," Maria said consolingly, "what is the reason for your visit. Should we be honoured?"

"Not at all, not at all," cried the Bishop, "we are just making enquiries but before we do that Maria my darling what about your famed hospitality? We haven't even got a glass yet that needs refilling. That rascal Brad is not hiding away again is he?"

"I'm here Father but the water of life isn't yet. I've had to send out. We had no stock," Brad interjected, "it'll be here soon."

"My goodness you must have been hitting it hard Brad," O'Halloran grumbled, "No stock! Unthinkable to an Irishman."

"I'm not Irish Father I'm an eyetie yankee," Brad replied with a smile, "with more than a hint of rebel. It's the mixture of garlic and olive oil. Absolutely lethal."

"So you'd better get down to business while you're waiting," Isabel suggested.

"Right," said the Bishop, suddenly serious, "this wedding now. Do we take it that it's another heathen one?"

Jeanette was immediately up in the air, "heathen!? I take it you are not, definitely not, talking about my marriage plans, right?"

"Unfortunately we are, Jeanette. Another one of the flock marrying outside the church," said the Reverend Father.

"One of the flock," shouted Jeanette, "one of the flock!! I'm a woman not a damn bird. Anyway I'm divorced. You don't recognise divorce so you couldn't marry me in the church anyway unless you wanted to support bigamy. So what's your problem?"

"The problem is that your husband to be is not a Catholic so your children maybe guided wrongly," said the Bishop.

"Well my very Catholic ex-husband was guided so well that he was a serial foul mouthed adulterer who lied the whole time he was with me," Jeanette cried, "my kids will be free to make up their own minds."

"Now, now," the Bishop said patronisingly, "within the Church all your sins can be forgiven and you can still reach salvation. Outside the Church you cannot."

"Well I can tell you your Grace that I won't forgive him and if you and God do then I don't want to achieve salvation. How could I live forever alongside that smarmy bastard. Hell would be Paradise in comparison."

"Bottoms up to that," said Brad, "cheers everyone."

"They're stoned are they, as punishment?
I didn't know drugs were legal there!"

The Value of Research

The family were at work. Their fishing fleet that had been at sea for a week or so was due in with a good catch.

The staff were ready.

The company sent refrigerated fish food all over the state and also had a fully operational cannery. They were not huge but were successful.

They were together in the office checking and rechecking schedules and equipment when a head poked round the door.

"Excuse me," said the head, "but nobody was out here so I just took the liberty of, er, you know?"

"Well," said Lance, "either stick your head outside again or bring the rest of your body in here with it."

"Oh," giggled the head, "okay then."

The head came further in followed by a long slim body.

The family looked enquiringly at a rather sheepish bespectacled young woman who looked enquiringly back at them.

"Yes, what is it?" asked Brad.

"What is what?" queried the young woman, seemingly mystified.

"What is it?" Brad asked again, emphasising the word it.

"What?" replied the young woman.

"We could do this all day," Mom chuckled, "see here young lady we want to know what it is you are doing here. That's what's what. Get it?"

"Oh I see," said the woman, "yes I see now."

"Great," exclaimed Lance, "then for heaven's sake get on with it, whatever it is. We're very busy. What is it you do?"

"I'm a researcher," said the woman, more convincingly than anything she'd said before, "I research things as to how and why and all that."

"Yeah right," Brad smirked, "do you want to research my sex life, sort of personal like?"

"Oh my goodness no!" exclaimed the researcher, "besides all that sort of thing's been done before."

"Yeah," laughed Isabel, "so much for truth eh? How can anyone be so stupid as to believe that people tell the truth about their sex lives? No one's ever told the truth about that in a million years. Only the liars will tell the truth. The researchers fell for it. They always fall for it."

"How about the one that found that if you watch strenuous sports on TV then you use up a lot of energy and can get fit. Turns couch potatoes into potential Olympic champions," Brad roared.

"What about the one that stated that cows fart litres of methane gas a day and actually measured the level of one fart," screamed Isabel, "how did they manage to do that and live? I mean one barn full of cows blew the whole place to smithereens. Whoever managed it surely deserves the Congressional Medal of Honour but I wouldn't want to be the one who presented it unless I was wearing a gas mask. Anyway Vegans and Vegetarians eat the same as cows don't they? So instead of saving the planet they are actually blowing it apart."

"Haven't I seen you before?" the researcher asked Isabel attempting to get back into the conversation.

"Nah," replied Isabel, "no chance, but research says that at any one time we all have six lookalikes in the world so it could have been one of my clones. You'll have to ask them when you see them."

The woman looked a bit blitzed but struggled on, "all very funny I'm sure but we do frequently present factual, useful information."

"Such as?" asked Mom.

"Well for instance I don't think you would dispute the findings that the average marriage produces 2.3 children in the Western World. Would you?"

"Nope," said Brad helpfully, "cos that explains how there are so many disabled people missing bits and pieces. If their parents had whole kids instead of 0.3 then they would be all right wouldn't they?"

There was silence for a moment as everyone looked at Brad who had the air of a scientist who had made a major break through. He had even ruffled his hair into a makeshift Einstein style.

He carried on, "Surely you're bright enough to know that what people say to you and what they actually do and believe can be two very different things.

Saddam Hussain, you remember him? Well he used to tell foreign journalists that every Iraqi loved him. When they expressed doubt he took them out, surrounded by bodyguards and secret police, and asked everyone in the street whether they loved Saddam. Every single person adored him. Of course they did - research proved it. Grow up girl."

After this learned discourse Brad was really puffed up, almost strutting.

"Research is useless unless it's useful," said Isabel, I mean useful for current propaganda. For instance my parents told me of a 1950's BBC TV live research programme, in black and white, set up to prove that drinking even small amounts of alcohol impaired driving ability. They lined up several drivers of varying ages and sex with different cars at a specially constructed course.

The course was quite difficult combining straight forward obstacles and complicated manoeuvres. They all tackled it stone cold sober in a reasonable period of time with few errors. They then relaxed and had a drink.

They tackled the course again completing it faster with fewer errors.

They had another drink and then another with similar results. The drivers improved. The organisers were getting frantic and abandoned the experiment. The programme was never repeated and hopefully lies shelved somewhere rather than being destroyed. You see the research contradicted the anti drink propaganda and that couldn't be allowed to prevail.

When you quote statistics you have to remember the joke of the famous Irish comedian who pointed out that nearly 15% percent of road accidents were caused by drunk drivers which showed that around 85% were caused by people completely sober. Therefore the boring sober guys should get off the road and leave it to the drunks.

If there are no drunk drivers then it means that 100% of all accidents are caused by non drinkers. A sobering thought that eh? Campaigning against drunk driving is fine but campaigning against drinking and driving is something else. That's an entirely different agenda."

Isabel paused for breath. For a moment she had morphed into Wunderwear Woman.

"Kid's can't drink in the USA until they are twenty one and it is vigorously enforced yet the gun laws are slack. So kids here can't drink but they can be killed with guns obtained easily by irresponsible screwed up other kids. In Europe it is different, the kids can drink but they are not often shot. So why not take away the guns from American kids and give 'em a drink. Needs thinking about eh!?

The researcher was naturally confused

The researcher was naturally confused and had been frantically searching either for a way in or a way out of the various conversations.

Lance came to the rescue, "sorry young lady, we are one of those normal dysfunctional families. We will all shut up for a while so we can hear why you are here. What research were you going to tell us about?"

"Well I wasn't, actually, I came to get some new business for my company and help you at the same time," she said breathlessly mixed with relief.

"And how were you going to do that exactly," asked Mom, admittedly a bit ominously.

"Well we could research your company's customers, track their needs, how they see things, whether they like what you do and all that," explained the researcher.

She was amazed when the family burst out laughing.

"Girl, we are not some high falutin' company with managers cut off from reality. We are face to face with our customers daily in a true market economy," laughed Mom, "we supply what they want, when they want at a price we both agree on. If that doesn't happen then they go somewhere else.

We don't need any fancy expensive company to tell us we need a fresh approach or a name change. Our customers tell us everything we need in no uncertain terms. Welcome to the workers of America. I think you had better go and try to impress the gamblers on Wall Street. They use other people's money, we have to use our own. We also have work to do. See ya fair lady."

Brad showed her to the door. She went quietly.

Who scares who?

Although all the future seemed to revolve around the coming wedding the business had to keep going forward irrespective.

During the peak tourist months when the well heeled Northerners headed South to avoid the freeze it was harder to attract unskilled labour into the smelly hands-on end of the fish business. The guys and gals preferred to work in service where the tips alone could outscore basic salaries.

Mom and Isabel handled the staffing and were generally careful in who they hired but they could never hope to be perfect especially in a state like Florida so open to welcome immigrants and refugees.

Every so often they were inspected unannounced by police, customs and immigration but had no problems as they were straightforward and transparent. If they had any bad guys on their staff then they wanted to know just as much as the authorities.

They had been very formally informed of a visit this time which was a little unusual. The inspections were supposed to come as a surprise, which they never were of course, so what was up with this one? Why the official notification?

FBI men in suits trying hard not to look like FBI men in suits!

All the family were on parade.

Oh oh, these were men in suits, not uniform. They were ultra serious, not at all informal.

They asked for the family's identification. The identification offered by the Suits was FBI. Good heavens they were FBI in suits trying too hard not to look like the FBI in suits.

What the hell!!??

One of the many benefits of Western civilisation and democracy is that the innocent have little to fear from authority because the authorities have to be answerable under law for their behaviour. Usually!!

However it is sensible to approach any enquiries in a sensible manner at least at first. Scream later if necessary.

The family were serious.

"Okay," said Lance, "why are you here? You can investigate all you like but we don't smuggle humans or drugs. We like a fair bit of booze but that's not illegal at our age. Investigate all you want but make it quick as we've a lot to get through today."

"I think you'd better understand that we don't want to disturb you folks unnecessarily but we are from the co-ordinated departments of the 'War on Terror' and we have had information regarding two members of your staff."

"Oh my gawd," shrieked Mom, "a terrorist investigation. Please don't say we are victims of a Fat One. Fat Ones are killers."

"Fatwa Mom," said Lance, "Okay gentlemen you've certainly got our attention, so why not tell us all about it and what you want to know."

"I can't," the agent said.

"Why not?" asked Isabel.

"Because it's top secret," said the agent.

"What's top secret?" asked Isabel.

"What we want to know," replied the agent.

Wunderwear was on to it, "if you can't tell us what you want to know, how can we tell you what you need to know you blockhead?" she shrieked.

"I can't tell you because I would possibly be betraying my country and exposing people to harm," the agent answered quite unperturbed.

"That's okay," laughed Wunderwear, "we will just ask a whistleblower. They don't care about anyone except their 15 minutes of fame and a large fortune. In fact they'll blow, sorry betray, any and everybody at the drop of a hat and run for it. Then they hide behind a less than friendly power pretending their feelings were hurt. They never do it for themselves of course, only to benefit the world but they actually undermine the very society they were supposed to protect. Insecure little shits if you ask me."

The agent opened his briefcase and showed a handful of photographs to the family.

"Do you recognise anyone in these photos," he asked, handing them around.

"Yes," said Brad, "that's me, that's Lance and that's Isabel."

"I didn't mean your family," the agent said exasperated, "I meant the rest."

"Oh sorry," said Brad, "I know the ones I know but don't know the others I don't know though."

"But you are standing alongside them," said the agent.

"So what," said Brad, "I'm standing next to you but I don't know you from Adam. What's your point?"

"We wondered if they spoke to you at all, about themselves, maybe their whereabouts. Can you recall anything at all?" the agent asked, looking hopefully around, "we checked and found they worked here. Still do apparently. So what are you hiding?"

"His brain as usual," Lance intervened. "sorry but we know all our staff and they are not any of these. They could have been part time workers that we take on temporarily in very busy periods so let's have a look at the records. Can you put names to faces?"

"Well, that's classified," said the agent, "afraid you don't have clearance."

Well then we can't clear you either can we because we don't do mug shots of our staff? So see you, bye," said Lance and turned away.

"Stop right there sir. This is a serious matter. Terrorism and terrorists are serious matters. Don't you want to stop them? Don't you want to save America and the American way of life?" the agent said firmly.

"Of course we do, we're not stupid, but this is?" exclaimed Wunderwear Woman, "we have enough to worry about without all this cloak and dagger stuff. Now either get on with it with us or get on your way without us. You're choice."

"We can get court orders to take anything we think we need, as well as virtually closing you down," said a large bull of a guy.

"Oh great," chortled Wunderwear, "threatening us now eh, so who's the terrorists? We are not the guilty ones, go and find the bad guys."

"That's what we are trying to do?" said the Bull, "but you stand in the way. We may have to reluctantly remove you."

"Jesus!" cried Mom, "to save America and the American way of life we're going to have to fight you. Is that it? Hey dumbo we are America and the American way of life. Get your brain out of your arse and ask us to co-operate, don't threaten us."

"Sorry Mam but we seem to have got off on the wrong foot," the first agent said, "you see we have names, their real names but they don't use them. We know what they look like but can't catch up on the names they're using now. They change them frequently as well as where they work and where they live.

We're not just trying to play catchup but also to try to get ahead."

"What's going on here," a soft voice said. It was Jeanette who had just arrived, "oh great, photos, I love photos. Can I have a look?"

She took them and surveyed them.

"Oh there's Ramon," she said, "what's he doing with Brad, not going drinking for sure as he doesn't drink and there's Artur with Lance. Said they were brothers. Didn't know you had these photos boys, when were these taken?"

There was dead silence.

Jeanette felt the atmosphere and shuffled uncomfortably.

"What's up?" she said, "have I said something wrong? They came by a couple of times last week looking for work. Real fresh they were, didn't only want work but wanted a date. Sent them packing. Told them to see Lance. Did you turn them down Bro'? They said they were living in an apartment just off Flagler Street downtown in Miami."

She stopped looking flushed and embarrassed.

"Can you tell us anymore, like in all you know?" said the Bull encouragingly.

"Who are you anyway," exclaimed Jeanette, "why should I tell you anything?"

"They are two of America's finest sis', you know 'Serve and Protect' just like the movies," Brad said helpfully.

"Well okay," she said slowly and doubtfully, "their surname was Hernando and they were Mexican immigrants but I never heard them speak Spanish and they looked more Middle East to me. They didn't drink, didn't smoke, didn't listen to pop or tex/mex but certainly were up for women. Eyeing them all the time. Said they come via Cuba, worked in and around Florida but wanted to be on or around the sea. Asked questions about boats, currents, inlets and all that. Joked about immigration and customs trying to sound me out but I told 'em to get lost. I had work to do. Saw them the other day working in that freight yard near where that big Carnival Cruise ship docks. They waved to me but I ignored them. That any good to you," she said hurriedly as Bull was already shouting into his communicator and moving away.

The family were left on their own in an instant.

"They never actually approached me," said Lance.

"Nor me," said Brad.

"Looks as though they may have thought about it and changed their minds when they saw you," Jeanette laughed, "I can understand that. You'd put anybody off. Even the fish turn their noses up at times."

The family went back to work.

So that was that they thought.

They thought wrong.

The Bull turned up two weeks later.

The family ushered him into the office out of the way.

"Thank you for your co-operation, we have tracked the suspects and would now appreciate your complete discretion and confidentiality as we wish to observe and not detain," he said importantly, "in the current climate we have to be absolutely sure that everything is watertight before we arrest and prosecute. Even then there are those who maintain that it is us who are guilty and the suspects who are innocent. So we require secrecy at this stage. I'm sure we can rely on you."

"OK, well we may not agree with every damn thing you do but we understand you are at least having a go," said Wunderwear, "I mean it's a favourite claim of terrorists who kill hundreds of innocent and guilty people alike that killing them only creates more terrorists. But what happens if we don't kill them?

That's what I want to know. Do ya reckon that there will be no more terrorists? Bullshit. Everyone will think they can get their own way through murder. Terrorists start the terror to get their cause known so they say and then complain about any and every retaliation. They try to make the victims feel guilty. One in a hundred causes are justified the rest are not."

"Go girl go!" thundered Mom, "let them go and justify a regime that denies women and children work, play and education through intimidation and cruelty. A regime that publicly and barbarically executes offenders, That tortures, mutilates and cripples men without beards. A regime closer to the devil than to god. That is intolerant and destructive of other forms of worship and destroys all opposition. A regime that cries foul in Abu Ghraib and Guantanamo over a bit of hardship and humiliation. And some suckers fall for it??!!"

"Yeah!" shouted Jeanette, "welcome to democracy. Perfect we ain't but we ain't them either."

"Not so sure about them there Republicans though," Mom said quietly.

"A word of warning," said the Suit, "you shouldn't use the word terrorist anymore."

"Why the hell not?" exclaimed Isabel.

"Apparently the terrorists don't like it, neither do their supporters. They think it's prejudicial. They hate the war on terror also. Gets them excited and all worked up. They say it makes them look bad and it upsets them. They say that it's not their fault that the world is in a mess."

"Jesus!" cried Wunderwear, "it may not be all their fault but they've gone a fucking long way down the line to make it worse. Nothing's ever their fault is it? They never look at themselves, they only look for excuses. Don't decide anything by discussion and compromise anymore. They say lets all blow ourselves and everyone else up in a fit of paddy because not everyone sees things the same way we do. It's not fair when you find new ways to stop us when we have found a great way to stop you. blah, blah, blah. If the attack on the Twin Towers wasn't war and it wasn't terror then what the bloody hell was it. Don't call them terrorists? Don't call it a war? Oh my goodness as if. What shall we call it? Ring a ring a roses?"

"Yeah gal, you tell 'em. Tell it as it is." Lance interrupted, "We are supposed to understand when they continually and intentionally blow up hundreds of innocent people with car bombs and suicide bombers but they can't understand how our smart bombs occasionally ain't so smart. Deliberately playing dumb I reckon. Smartarses all of 'em. At least we tried to give em a taste of freedom and democracy. They need to get their shit together and sort themselves out not us."

"Huh! They take the piss out of us for saying that we have nothing against the ordinary people as though we're hypocrites who know nothing and mean something else," said Wunderwear, "but the ordinary people have nothing against us either unless they're wound up by fanatics or politicians. They want to live in peace and security like everyone else. If they didn't they'd all be suicide bombers wouldn't they, millions of them?"

"Yeah, if they all did that, I mean say even a billion of them taking two of us with them then we'd still here, they wouldn't and we would have solved the terrorist problem and the world overpopulation situation in one go," Brad said in all seriousness, "we can't win can we? If we ignore or deal with nasty regimes we're wrong and if we fight them and depose them we're wrong. I reckon we're all right pal."

"Oh god, he's gone again," said Jeanette.

"Yeah we're all right," agreed Mom, "but dunno about the Republicans though."

They patted each other on the back and agreed to maintain silence.

They couldn't guarantee it of course. Not for long but Bull was happy enough.

Automated

Lance called a family meeting.

"I've got a couple of guys coming one morning to look at what we do. They're work study experts who tell you ways of cutting costs and improving your business. Let's see what they have to say. Okay?"

"You telling us that we've got total strangers coming in here, nosing around," asked Mom managing to make her question sound like a threat, "they don't come cheap. How much do these two so called experts cost then?"

"Ah," exclaimed Lance somewhat triumphantly, "they cost nothing. First assessments free. Can't be fairer than that can it?"

"Yep it can. It would be fairer if they didn't come at all," said Mom, "can you just imagine what our people will make of it? They'll be thinking sellouts, takeovers, layoffs, wage cuts and shutdowns and that's just the ones who can think. God help the rest off 'em."

"So what," said Brad, "it's our company ain't it? We make the decisions don't we? They're nothing without us."

"And where are we without them?" asked Isabel, "you're the first to complain when we can't get enough workers. The fish would go rotten."

"Yeah," cried Jeanette shrilly, "we're a family company, hands on. We work with them, they work with us. Too many companies forget that. They treat staff as though they're furniture, assets or liabilities on a ledger sheet and they call themselves managers. Phooey!"

"That's why we need to consider automation," Lance said evenly, "look how workers move on, robots don't. Workers get tired and sick, robots don't. Workers make mistakes, robots don't. Needs thinking about."

"Hold it right there, Please think about it," said Isabel in great danger of sliding into Wunderwear, "robots don't eat, drink, wear or buy what they make. Humans do. So if the objective is to make the whole workforce unemployed what is the point of robots making anything.?"

"They can make more faster and better," said Brad.

"If that's so why not keep most of the workforce on with less hours in a supervisory capacity," Wunderwear asked reasonably, "you produce more and sell more at a sensible price because more people are in work. They will have more leisure time to go shopping. There are more taxpayers, less benefit claims and a more balanced budget."

"Wow! That's original," exclaimed Jeanette.

"Not really," laughed Wunderwear, "this was discussed years ago but greed and selfishness took over. Modern managers take a parochial view. Micro brains in a macro complex society."

"Didn't your Maggie Thatcher say there was no such thing as society," asked Brad with a smug expression.

"Of course, what did you expect from a mediocre grocer's daughter with delusions of grandeur," Wunderwear chuckled, "she said a lot more stupid things as well along with her pal Ronnie, the B movie actor. Frightening isn't it when you think of those who actually get into positions of power and even more scary when you realise that in a democracy we vote for them."

"Well I think we should still see what they have to say," said Mom, "we need to keep up even if we don't like it. But I must say my heart is with Isabel and her Wunderwear Woman feelings. We left an Italy we felt offered us little and came here and got on well. Because of our background we have always treated our workers as well as possible and not treated them as slaves. It hasn't always been appreciated but mostly we have been highly regarded because of our fairness and not just because of our money and position. In the old days the big bold industrial barons created product and work but hated paying for it. Now we have a techno revolution that puts people out of work and they still don't want to pay. There's something wrong. Society, whether it exists or not, needs to grow up. Either stop breeding and let the human race die out or face up to responsibilities and live and work together on a more equal basis."

"Right on Mom," exclaimed Wunderwear, "when you over favour minorities you can prejudice the attitude of the majority and really piss them off. When you give too much freedom and licence to some then you deny it to others maybe more deserving. Don't force an issue unless you want to force a resistance unless the resistance is unjust."

"Okay, enough, enough!" cried Lance, "for fuck's sake I just wanted a free outside opinion about what we do and how we do it. I didn't want a Capitol Hill discussion on the future of mankind. I want to sell fish, not win a Nobel Prize. Can we get on."

"They don't give a Nobel prize for fishing do they?" asked Brad.

"Oh mah gawd, he's gone again," laughed Jeanette, "when do these guys come? When they due?"

"Tomorrow," Lance said, "we leave 'em alone to go round and see for themselves."

They did.

Within minutes Lance was faced with a staff deputation.

The first gambit was one of co-operation and worries about security.

"Hey boss, what's going on? Two industry spies got past security and are sticking their noses in everywhere. Dewayne was going to do them over but we thought we'd see you first. Want us to forcibly evict them?"

"Nah," said Lance, "they're just checking us out. A sort of inspection if you like. It's okay."

"They ain't in uniform and they ain't got badges," noted the receiving supervisor with a change of attitude, "so how's it okay? Something going on we should know about?"

"Something fishy you mean," Brad laughed out loud but nobody else joined in.

Mom flashed him a warning glance so he subsided with a wounded air.

"No," said Lance, "we bin doin' things the same way for years, stood us in good stead but we thought an outside look would do no harm. See if we need changes."

"Yeah changes for us you mean, like in layoffs," said Old Bill from packing.

"No," said Mom, "like in maybe changes but no layoffs. No one will lose their jobs, you have my word on that."

"That's what they all say. Then boom bang all gone. Everyone knows that bosses say the opposite," said the supervisor, "look at sports managers. The worst thing that can happen is that the board issue a statement assuring them of their continued support and confidence. Two days later they gone man. Change is the kiss of death for poor guys."

"Poor guys, poor guys," cried Isabel, "poor you are not. Even Old Bill drives a German Car. You know one of those models that the makers don't have to recall in their thousands to rectify defects. I reckon that America and Japan are having a contest leading to 'Total Recall'. Arnie Schwarzenneger to reprise motor cars. Who out of you lot lost their homes in the recent recession?"

"You got nothing to worry about," Jeanette interjected quietly, "we are a family business and as long as there are fish in the sea and people to eat what we catch then you are family. If we have to do a few things differently then who cares?"

"Yep," said Brad, trying to work his way back in, "who knows. Maybe Old Bill will be gutting instead of packing."

"Careful my knife don't slip," he replied," at my age I'm not so sure of the target. Hate to cut off your gills young man."

"Are we done here people?" asked Lance, "we got strangers roaming around wondering why half the work force has gone awol. Thank you."

The deputation wandered away muttering.

A few weeks later the report came in. It recommended either near total automation at fantastic expense or a few changes for the sake of change.

The automation removed the flexibility of taking on and laying off part time labour at critical times, ensured constant product flow even at slow times and took little account of fish being a very perishable commodity. The family were faced with either huge expansion at one go whatever the level of business or building up slowly with a more flexible approach to their market over time.

They chose the slower route but changed some of the staff around just to make a point. Old Bill didn't get to gut any fish though and Brad kept his gills.

Ol' Bill didn't get to gut any fish and Brad managed to keep his gills.

The Arrivals

The Australians were due to arrive. The family weren't exactly sure who and how many were coming but they didn't care. All would be welcome. American hospitality. Forget the gooks, ginks and headlines - just look at the ordinary decent people for a change. If all Americans were as dumb as Duck Dynasty they would never have put a man on the moon. One day the Americans will wake up to how they too often portray themselves around the world. Most would be horrified. What they probably saw at home as a bit of harmless fun or sentimental concern didn't look the same when exported.

Jeanette was most excited. She hadn't seen her fiancee for several months and had missed him badly.

They all met up at a local hotel.

Russ and Jeanette just smothered each other in kisses, holding each other so close and wriggling together so sensuously that Brad coloured purple and had to go to the bathroom. He was there quite a while.

When he finally emerged Lance asked, "hello brother, you took your time, once wasn't enough eh?"

Brad thought about it, turned round and went back.

It didn't matter much as Russ and Jeanette were only just disentangling themselves. They still appeared hungry.

Mom was shocked, not with her daughter but with Brad.

"I worry about that boy," she exclaimed, "we are not voyeurs, we don't want second hand sex, we want the real thing and bless these two kids, they are up for it. That's what I call healthy. Brad should wait his turn. He's never been right since he took up with that fancy English girl and all her smart friends in New York. Go and get him Lance, would you?"

"No way Mom," laughed Lance, "he's big enough and ugly enough to hold his own thank you very much. Let him finish, I'm not bringing him out here half done. Too messy! Let's just introduce ourselves."

They did.

Russ proudly but a little self-consciously introduced his mother and father, sister and brother. His friends, Dave and Pete, who had met them originally in Florida some time ago were not able to make it but would meet up with them in Australia. Mum was the solid down to earth type while Dad was tall and spare. His sister Susie was one of those lovely free and easy Oz girls and his brother Cooper looked as though he surfed all day.

There was no uneasiness.

Wunderwear mused, "these are straightforward ordinary people like us who get on well enough everyday all over the world until we're told by our superiors that we are really enemies. It's our own bloody fault that we believe them and disbelieve them all at the wrong times. We compound the errors of our leaders. Nutcases all of us."

They are just straightforward, ordinary people like us who get on well enough everyday all over the world until told by our superiors that they are enemies.

Mom, as always was great. She often thought wrong but said it right, unlike Isabel who when under the influence of Wunderwear Woman often thought right but said it wrong.

Brad however didn't know the difference.

"Welcome," he said, "what does it feel like to be the right way up for a change? Must be awkward hanging upside down down under all the time."

There was a short silence, followed by weak grins. This puzzled Brad who thought he was making polite conversation. "I mean if it wasn't for gravity you'd fall off wouldn't you? It's okay for us as we're the right way up you see.

We'd just fall down but you'd fall off wouldn't you?"

"This way to the bar folks," interrupted Lance, chuckling as though Brad was trying to be funny. "God help us if they think he's serious," he muttered to Isabel, "they'll be hopping away faster than the kangaroos."

While relaxing and drinking the conversation switched to Susie and Cooper.

Cooper was an air traffic controller at Brisbane Airport. When a student he had served a period as a beach lifeguard. These were really hard, tough guys and gals, brave and selfless. Mum was glad he gave it up to get what she called a proper job.

When a student he had served a period as a beach
lifeguard. Hard, tough, selfless guys and gals.

Susie was an engineer, working in Robotics.

"Not much difference between Robots and most humans now is
there?" said Isabel, feeling tempted to slide into Wunderwear guise,
"millions of people going through the same old motions and routine
day after day. Must be on time, must perform, mustn't lose focus."

"You're right there," smiled Susie, "trouble is people feel pain and
resentment, have emotions, robots don't. Some researchers want
to see if that can be duplicated but I don't see the point when most
doctors and nurses are working to relieve it."

"Yeah but love and lust is different eh girl," cried Wunderwear, "the
best way to relieve that is to get some and then get some more! Don't
give it to the robots no matter how real they may look."

Susie was one of those lovely free and easy Oz girls.

"Why not? Sounds good to me," shouted Brad, "if you could make 'em more active than a blow up plastic Marilyn Monroe I'd be first in the queue. My Marilyn goes all soggy and squashy after a session of passion. Needs more air. Gives new meaning to a blow job."

"I don't think Susie's working on that Brad," said Lance, "so I'd stick with your Marilyn if I was you. But anyway I thought you had Jayne Mansfield."

"Yeah I have," Brad smirked, "I've got them both. I like two in a bed sometimes."

Mom promptly switched to the topic of the wedding.

She was more comfortable with what she viewed as a heathen wedding as she had received notice that her two long time Catholic stalwarts Bishop Clancy and The Reverend Father O'Halloran were being promoted and transferred to Boston. Mom didn't fancy unknown latin priests offering their opinions. They would have to be bedded in first and proven before being listened to.

The families agreed on a beach wedding. Cooper was best man and Lance would give Jeanette away.

All was arranged and went off with only a few hitches. Lance performed handsomely so did Cooper. Mom and Mum cried as expected while Brad, as usher, did his bit for unity by completely mixing up guests of the bride and the guests of the groom. Nobody knew each other and nobody cared which worked out just fine.

The reception was a barbecue and disco on the sand.

The bar was a long one and open to anyone.

It seemed that it was also open to everyone.

Mom and Isabel were making sure the food was kept flowing well and the booze not so well when they noticed a young girl studying the buffet intently but also somewhat critically.

"You okay dear?" asked Mom, "made up your mind yet?"

"Not really," the girl answered, "there's too much living stuff here. A lot of animals died to cover this table."

"Make up your mind," Isabel laughed, "living or dead, I don't see much moving about here, do you?"

"It doesn't have to move, does it?" the girl snapped impatiently, "it's the emotion isn't it? Before an animal dies it experiences fear and when I eat that animal then I eat it's fear. Chemicals you know? I don't want to inherit that fear."

"You alright girl?" asked Wunderwear, "you daft or something? If that was true then lions, tigers and crocodiles would be scared shitless wouldn't they?

They frighten the living daylights out of their prey first and often tear it to pieces while still alive. They'd love this table and wouldn't have anything like a nervous breakdown afterwards. They'd be licking their lips. Get your brain in gear. You're still young so there's a chance for you."

"You don't sniff glue or anything do you young lady?" asked Mom, "it plays tricks on your mind you know."

"What you talkin' about?" exclaimed the girl, looking confused and embarrassed.

"Take it easy Mom," said Wunderwear, "this girl's so naive she thinks that selotape is a glue sniffers fast food take away."

"Oh I hate you," snapped the girl and she ran away.

"Were we a bit hard on her, do you think?" asked Mom quietly, "she said she hates us."

"Nah," said Wunderwear, "just a favourite expression when they can't think of a sensible reply. Kids her age change their minds every five minutes. She'll have forgotten it already."

"Do you think so?" asked Mom, "she's heading back this way crying with a grim looking guy in tow."

"Ah well, stand firm, straighten up and look determined," said Wunderwear.

"We could run," said Mom, "he looks tough."

"Oh come on Mom," laughed Wunderwear, "I've seen more life in a pair of old socks."

Mom had to laugh.

Bad timing.

The guy pulled up in front of them, chest heaving trying to get his breath back.

"What's so funny?" he gasped, "You think it's funny upsetting my little girl? Two fatsos like you picking on a kid."

Mom just about held back Wunderwear.

"If I were you I'd beat it before she tears you to pieces," said Mom, "she eats meat and doesn't digest the fear."

"Huh?" what you on about," snarled the man.

"You don't know then talk to your kid," shouted Wunderwear, "do you ever talk to her?"

"Yes he does, all the time when he's not in jail," cried the girl.

"You been to jail?" Mom exclaimed, "more than once?"

"Yeah, I was innocent. I got caught for things I didn't do," he said defiantly.

"That's right," said Lance who had just arrived, "Hi Earl. Earl here definitely got caught for things he didn't do. On one break-in he didn't remove his finger prints after the robbery, another time in a supermarket he didn't put on his face mask and on a bank job he didn't notice the cameras. You're right Dude you got caught okay for things you didn't do. Like going straight."

"Well this is a wedding so the food and drink is free. You weren't invited but you're welcome," said Mom, "but talk to your girl properly if you can, she's a bit screwed up. Go on, get stuck in." They did.

Mom and Isabel were walking away when the girl ran round them with a kebab in one hand and a coke in the other.

"I get all my info from the internet you know," she said knowledgeably standing full square in front of them, "Tells you everything you want to know. It's more cool than school."

"Yeah great," replied Isabel, "but if it's all so fab why is it so slow and complicated?"

"Cos it isn't," said the girl cockily, "you even have computer controlled cars. You know, for adults like."

"God help us then," laughed Isabel, "look if I want to stop and turn off my car then that's what I do. Great in an emergency. What happens if you want to turn off your computer? You go to turn off and press turn off. It then asks you if you want to turn off your computer and you say yes. It then asks you if you really want to turn off your computer and if you say yes then there is a number of secs delay."

"It's the same with remove trash. By the time you finally remove it you've forgotten what you want to do. Heaven help my car. By the time I convince it to stop I've already crashed or gone past where I want to go. Imagine saying 'okay car, stop now or else we crash' and the car says 'do you want to stop now?' and I say 'yes I do' and the car says 'do you really want to stop now?' and I scream 'yes stop now' and the car says 'I will automatically stop in fifty seconds.' No way girl, when I trust myself to a synthetic brain then I know I've gone mad."

"People do and will though," smirked the girl.

"Look you're too young to parachute but let me tell you this. There is a pressure device on your reserve chute which should open automatically if you reach a certain velocity when your main chute doesn't open due to problems.

If you are conscious and do not release your reserve yourself then you will not jump again. Anyone who trusts their life to a mechanical or electronic device instead of their training is viewed as unfit to jump. Get it?"

"Sort of," said the girl, "dunno what that's to do with a car though."

"Simple," said Isabel, "no one's going to allow you to drive a computer controlled car unless you've first passed a test proving you can handle a normal car well in the first place. What happens to you if the computer fails and you don't know what to do?"

"What?"

"You die young lady, you die," Isabel chuckled, "there are automatic pilots in aircraft but every pilot has to know how to fly without one. What happens when your computer breaks down or goes off line?"

"What happens?" asked the girl.

"You go to school which is where you should have been in the first place," Isabel cried, "get it now?"

I get all my info from the internet - it's more cool than school.

"Not really but the kebab is great," said the girl as she walked away, "I'm really into meat now."

"Young lady, listen to me," said Mom with one of those stern adult looking no nonsense expressions on her face, "you're young, with all the opportunities before you, don't waste them. You have your whole life in front of you."

"Yeah, I know, so there's no hurry then is there. It's not as though I'm old like you and gotta rush to fit things in is it?" she answered, "everyone asks me what I want to do with my life as though I should know at fifteen. I know what I don't want and how to avoid it but I'm not sure what I do want and how to get it. Is that a crime or something?"

"Oh come on," said Isabel, "Life is wonderful. Humans and animals are incredible and capable of great things aren't they? What about you?"

The girl wasn't really interested. She looked alive when looking at the food but had sort of dulled down during this conversation. She seemed to have heard it all before and probably had.

"Humans are I suppose, can do all sorts, but animals get pretty boring after a time," she mused, "I mean they just do the same old thing, don't they? Wow, like, elephants never forget and trundle around in a mob but they're never gonna do the pole vault are they? Cheetahs can run fast but they'll never compete in Formula One and as for Lions well they're pretty frightening even eating and sleeping but they're never gonna win a grand slam at tennis. As for lizards how the hell are they gonna get to the moon let alone develop enough to be space invaders. What sort of an idiot is it who makes nearly every earth invader a slobbering lizard? Kids would never think up crap like that. The dinosaurs are cool but they didn't hang about did they? They would have made the humans really perform. Sorry, gotta go now. See ya," and she wandered off along the beach.

Mom and Isabel looked at each other and said the inevitable, "kids ain't what they used to be. Dunno what the world's gonna be like with them in charge."

They both nodded with serious intent expressions.

The girl glanced back at them. "My god, adults are really weird. I hope I don't grow up to be one of them! Nah, no chance. No wonder the world's in a mess."

With that re-assuring thought she wandered on lost in her own world of daydreams where she triumphs overall just like Wonder Woman.

The Arrangements

The two families were standing together at the end of the day in general agreement that it had been a good one. They filled their glasses. Russ and Jeanette were mulling over Brad's speech, the jury still being out as to whether it was fun or a fuck up. He had decided to pour out his heartfelt sympathy for his sister over her first disastrous marriage and share it with the whole reception. The fact that Jeanette's ex husband had been in the crowd hadn't helped especially when the ex had jumped to his feet and told everyone that he had been trying to escape the smell of fish. He had appealed to everyone trying to gain sympathy and when that seemed to strike a chord he went further. "With more than six billion people on this planet washing their shit daily into the ocean who wants to eat fish anyway," he shouted.

That did it. Lance leaped around the table and ran flat out at him. The ex tried to dodge and then decided to make a run for it. He only succeeded because a friend stuck out a foot and Lance tripped over it. The smug look on the friend's face disappeared under a right uppercut coming as Lance shot up off the floor. The blow connected with the button on his chin and his smile seemed to move up higher than his nose. Brad rushed to calm him down only to spend time dodging the angry punches from Lance who blamed his brother for the whole thing.

The guests applauded and appreciated the diversion far more than the speeches. It was only then that they noticed that the bridegroom was missing. Search parties were despatched.

Russ was found banging the head of the ex husband repeatedly against the trunk of a tree.

Some guests were a bit worried but Jeanette reassured them that no amount of battering would make the slightest difference. She knew from experience that he was a thick male chauvinist pig. That type never learned she said.

So everyone went back to the reception firmly of the opinion that every wedding should have a punch up to relieve the monotony of gooey insincere speeches.

Bishop Clancy and the Reverend Father O'Halloran were heard telling everyone that it had made them feel at home. In Ireland no wedding was complete without a fight and sentimental sing song. It's what made Ireland what it was.

On the back of that so many guests decided there and then to visit Ireland that the Irish Tourist Board considered making it the central theme of their adverts.

In the end they kept the sentimental songs but substituted Leprechauns instead of a fracas. They figured that tourists would rather spend longer searching for the little people than getting into a fight.

Brad thought that was a pity.

He was also a little bit sad that the day was over. All those beautiful girls and he hadn't bothered to get a date or a phone number. He wanted a replay.

"Don't worry Bro-in-Law," Russ told him, "look, the whole world is full of beautiful women and great looking guys. Vanity is nutsville man. As one gorgeous guy or girl goes round that corner full of themselves another one comes round this one, just as full of themselves. You know the drill. Look at me and gasp, aren't I beautiful? Yeah get real. Beauty isn't only skin deep, it's more superficial than that. Just be cool man."

"What about me then?" asked Isabel, "I've never been a beauty and I've got a lot of skin."

"Listen my darling, my angel," chuckled Lance, "you've always been a beauty. You've slimmed a lot now but you've always gone in and out in the right places and had an hour glass figure. You just needed a lot of glass and the Sahara desert to fill it."

He had to be quick on his feet. Isabel may have been laughing but the punches were deadly.

Brad looked at Russ's sister with a sloppy misplaced grin, "okay sis, what about you? I bet you like 'em rough and tough. Me, I'm a bum, tit and leg man."

"No surprises there then," she laughed, throwing back her head and tossing her hair. Normally a very corny action but everyone had drunk buckets and so found it attractive, in fact so many buckets that it seemed really attractive, "However I am cerebral."

"Oh my gawd, do you want a black coffee or something?" Brad exclaimed, "do you need to sit down?" He looked round for help.

"Dumbo," whispered Lance in his ear, "she means she looks above the neckline. She likes brain not brawn."

"What a waste of a girl like that," mused Brad.

Russ's parents had gone to that lovely relaxed place that a sufficient quantity of alcohol induces. Too much and you lose it, too little and you don't get it. They were there. They were so happy they wanted to invite everyone in sight to Australia.

Clancy and O'Halloran sensibly refused pleading other duties and Jeanette's ex, even though still suffering from nearly having his head bashed in, had enough wit to politely turn down the offer. Jeanette was amazed at his politeness. She hadn't seen it before. Perhaps Russ and the tree had knocked some sense into him.

Earl was delighted until Russ told him that jailbirds weren't welcome down under. Something sensitive to do with history apparently. Lance reminded himself to check it out sometime.

They all looked around.

Where was Cooper?

He had made his speech as Best Man. He reckoned that it was time his brother Russ gave up sheep shagging and got down to the real thing. Russ shouted out that, "sheep shagging was the real thing wasn't it? Just ask the Kiwis. Why did you think they got so many sheep in NZ?"

One New Zealander stated that it was certainly better than trying to shag dingos or Skippies. Sheep seemed grateful. Gays shouldn't try to get it up the back of rams though. They definitely weren't grateful. Gave getting the horn a different meaning.

Cooper tried to bring some order back but one of his pals said with great enthusiasm that his preference was for heifers. He then got into deeper water by explaining that he meant women. His partner shook up a bottle of champagne and let him have it full on. That got everyone going and alcohol was soon flying all over the place. Brad was bobbing, weaving and jumping around in an attempt to catch every last drop.

The rest of Cooper's speech was lost in the slow calm down. It remained that way for a while until Brad was moved to stand up and make his offering which caused the fight.

Everyone had a good time.

Mom was not too sure exactly what it had all been about. Everything was rosy. She had fondly been working her way through her bottles of Italian red wine, Ruffino Chianti in the straw basket called a Fiasco. Seemed appropriate! Lance and Isabel had got them especially for her and she didn't like to tell them that she really preferred her more basic roots of vino da tavola or table wines. However she never turned down an Amerone or a Barolo if someone else was paying.

But what had happened to Cooper.

The last time he had been seen was on the dance floor waggling his hips while two girls rubbed themselves all over him, up and down, back to front.

He hadn't been seen since.

The families hung around slowly finishing off a few drinks when Cooper came into sight holding up three girls.

"Yeah!" laughed Russ, "that's my brother, he's that kind of guy."

When Cooper let them go the girls slowly sank down on the ground. They went into a supportive huddle with dissatisfied false smiles all over their faces.

They were ignored.

Thoughts came back to post wedding activities.

The arrangements were made.

The bride and groom along with Russ's family would go home to Oz near Brisbane. Isabel's crowd would follow on a little later arriving first in Brisbane, staying on the Gold Coast before going up to Cairns and the Great Barrier Reef to get a bit of the wild before going onto civilisation around Sydney.

Australia wasn't just a country, it was a continent and like America had so many spectacular, beautiful, scenic varieties of nature. More than can ever be imagined. The country as a whole was less hospitable than the USA, meaning that the most tolerable life could be enjoyed mainly around the coastal regions while the insects seemed more vicious than anywhere else on earth. A visit to an outside dunny was fraught with danger. The insects found the early immigrants easier than the early immigrants found employment. The insects also took to their new surroundings quicker than the immigrants.

On a continent of unusual creatures the most unusual of course was the white man. He still is. He got there millions of years after everything else had survived and flourished and then acted as though he owned the place. Just like America actually!!?? Well they didn't know better then, or so they say.

The family decided against going via Europe. Mom didn't feel up to visiting family. She reckoned she had enough to do accommodating new ones without having to meet up with old ones.

So they went via Hawaii.

They didn't stop over though.

Up and Over Down Under

They all tumbled and stumbled off the plane looking exactly as though they had been travelling for a hours.

They made their way to immigration, lined up and attempted to organise themselves. All passports and visas were in order so they expected no problems and were determined to cause none.

This was not true of the tall lumbering Abraham Lincoln type character in front of them. He ignored the yellow "Wait Here" line, stood up close to the passenger already at the desk, looked over and down on him, scrutinising what was going on. Possibly just an over curious type but it didn't suit the immigration official.

"Excuse me sir," he said in a stern official voice, "step back behind the yellow line please."

Abraham Lincoln just grunted but didn't move.

The official instructed him again more impatiently.

"Step back behind the yellow line please sir."

"Why?" asked Abraham.

"What do you mean, why?" exclaimed the officer, "because I say so, that's why."

"Why?" came the same question to the new statement.

"You have to give some privacy to the people in front of you, give them some space," said the official, "avoid making them feel uncomfortable."

"Oh I see," said Abraham turning to the passenger being interviewed, "am I making you uncomfortable?"

"No, actually," laughed the passenger.

"See," explained Abraham, "no one's uncomfortable, so what's the problem?"

The officer over theatrically laid down some papers and shifted others, slowly rose to his feet and came round the counter to stand on the yellow line.

"I am a custodian of the borders of this country and I instruct you to stand here now," he said, "now sir if you please."

Abraham did so but took his time.

The officer returned to his desk, dealt with the passenger up front, occasionally checking on the position of Abraham who hadn't moved, and then called out next.

Abraham didn't move.

"Next," shouted the official. "That's you sir," looking at Abraham.

"Are you sure?" he drawled, looking loftily all over, "wouldn't want to make anyone uncomfortable now, would I, especially a custodian of Australia's erstwhile border?"

The family looked at him in part admiration and part shock. He was never going to get in. But he did.

However.

Customs took him apart even before he had collected his bags. They were checking his hand luggage and questioning everyone else.

Isabel asked what all the fuss was about.

A Customs officer explained, "Australia has been a separate continent for millions of years and has developed unique flora and fauna which has to be protected. We don't allow any non indigenous species to come in. We quarantine and destroy anything that can be viewed as dangerous to the native species. New Zealand wisely does the same."

Isabel couldn't help herself. Wunderwear Woman came roaring out.

"Bit late for that isn't it? Native species my arse! You've had bloody sailors, soldiers, settlers and immigrants thumping around for centuries bringing plants, pets, animals and god knows what with them and god knows how much junk is thrown up on your shores yet you worry about a jar of honey. I reckon you've already done all the damage that can be done. Remember rabbits and myxomatosis?"

The officer looked a bit bemused but chose to regard it as a joke. "we do our best to protect what we've got now," he said.

Shortly after this a plain clothes young man approached Isabel while waiting at the baggage carousel.

"Can I ask you why you are visiting my country," he said quietly.

"Can you tell me whose asking and why you are so bloody nosey," said Wunderwear.

"Yes, I am with National Security," he said flashing a card and badge.

"Look mate, I can buy stuff like that in any store in the states along with a uniform, which you aren't wearing by the way," cried Wunderwear, "and if you think that I am any sort of a threat to your country and security then you are not up to the job pal. Go and sit behind a desk. But as you ask I am here to meet the family of the Australian guy who has just married the sister of my husband. We're not going to put buckets on our heads and pretend we're the Ned Kelly Gang. Are you up to working that one out?"

The guy walked away.

"What is it with this place? For goodness sake let's get free of the officials and meet some real people. Bloody hell trying to get into the country is like competing in the Krypton factor," she said to Lance who had missed most of the encounters while looking out for the luggage. He looked puzzled but just got on with organising the bags and trolleys.

"You were a bit hard on them in there weren't you?" he asked a little perplexed, "they're only doing their job you know. Following instructions."

"That's the problem," said Isabel, "it's an excuse for anything and everything. Only obeying orders. Isn't that what the Nazis said? Putting in the odd polite sir or madam doesn't make it different. In England we call those people Jobsworth. Those who say I can't be human and normal, it's more than my jobs worth. Give some people authority and they can't see common sense anymore. They go over the top. A bit of suspicion's one thing but going on and on at times just seems spiteful. Here in Oz it's hilarious. They sanctimoniously refuse people with criminal records entry now but more than half the original settler population was descended from so called felons. Where's the humanity? They're not really that ignorant, they're educated right enough but it's selective. Selective history and selective memory. That's the real disease of religions and politics."

They finally got clear and met the real Australians.

They were waiting in the arrivals hall obviously very excited.

Hugs, kisses, air kisses and introductions were flying all over the place and not all within the two families. Everybody seemed happy to see everyone else.

"Who cares?" thought Isabel, "people are just people the world over until some lousy bastard winds them up. There are pricks everywhere of course but too many seem to find their way to the top. I don't wanna be on the bottom though, middle to higher suits me fine." She sighed.

Isabel had seen some of the bottom and it looked bad, even from the top down. Goodness only knows what it looked like from the bottom up. Like any sensible young woman she preferred not to experience it personally but that didn't stop her feeling a burning sense of injustice and sympathy for the underprivileged. She was determined to stick up for them whenever and wherever necessary.

She was happily married, thoroughly capable, intelligent and also very tough.

She only had a brother. Both her parents had died a few years previously but she had married into a great family of disparate characters. Brad was somewhat of a loose cannon. In spite of having a great mom he was in no hurry to marry. He preferred to play the field. He was of the opinion that the real penalty for bigamy was having two mothers in law. When the doctor told him to give up smoking, get more exercise and jog say two or three miles each day he phoned in after being missing for a week asking to be collected twenty miles from home.

Isabel loved him. They all did. He gave up smoking.

They collected themselves and everyone else and moved out.

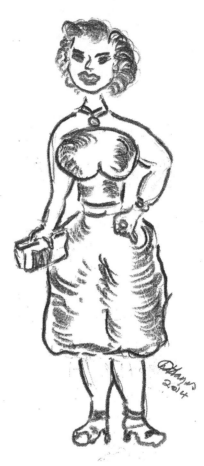

I don't want to be on the bottom though. Middle to higher suits me just fine.

Black Out

They checked into their hotel on the seafront on the Gold Coast, a not too long drive from Brisbane. Miles of beautiful golden sandy beaches.

They were recommended to use Brisbane airport when flying although Coolengatta was much closer.

Russ explained that Coolengatta airport was more of a bus stop than an airport.

The planes came in, roared round, didn't switch off engines, even when passengers were disembarking, and according to how many got off then that's how many got on. If you missed then you waited for the next one. They came in from all directions and flew off in the same way. Not bad if you were on your own but not with a crowd. The chances of staying together were slim.

It was fun but uncertain.

The family took notice.

First off they spent the first few days on the beach.

It was like Baywatch. The Aussie lifeguards were in superb condition. Brad was crosseyed looking at the girl's buns. There was so much choice he couldn't chose. Cooper promised to help him out when he took some time off in a few days.

Brad felt the need to explain a few things first.

"Look man," he said earnestly, "I'm impressed with these great young girls but I've gotta say I fancy them older."

"No probs," said Cooper, "whatever turns you on. When you say older, what sort of older?"

"Well, like, older," Brad stuttered, "I mean more than younger."

"That's not a bloody lot of help mate, is it?" laughed Cooper, "give me a bit more to go on, will ya?"

"You see I reckon that once a woman passes thirty six or so she's over the hill, past her prime, running out of sell by date, sort of thing, Brad said awkwardly, "she knows it, sees younger, better looking gals coming up behind her and it makes her 'ornery. Know what I mean?"

"Not quite sure pal," answered Cooper, "are you saying that you want them a bit older but younger than thirty six or what?"

"Nah I want them older and 'ornery," Brad chuckled, "makes 'em easier to dump when I get tired of 'em. The older they get the more neurotic and paranoid they are. Around sixty they seem to have got over it but before that they seem in a state of permanent pms. Can't live with them so that's why their husbands dump 'em. That's why women go into business. They can take it out on everyone else."

Wunderwear Woman was listening in.

She interrupted quietly but dangerously, "Brad when I reach thirty six I will talk to you again about this and if you are still saying the same thing I will kill you."

Brad laughed uneasily, "no you won't Sis, I know you don't mean it."

"Oh but I do," shouted Wunderwear, "because by then I really will be neurotic and paranoid through having to deal with pricks like you for years."

Brad looked at Cooper, shrugged his shoulders and said, "well whatever."

"Yeah, okay mate, see what I can do," Cooper grinned, "see if I can find a Glamorous Grannie or two just for you. There's plenty out early morning walking their dogs. Can't sleep you see, nothing to keep 'em in bed. They all wear designer clothes that the kids would love to wear but can't afford. Would look a whole lot better on'em than on wrinkles, sags, facelifts, botox and lipposucks."

"Right," Wunderwear exclaimed, "that's two of you dead before pensionable age,"

"Come off it, I'm just messing about," cried Cooper, "so is Brad, ain't he?"

"I'm not. Are you?" said Brad, very disappointed, "You'd got me going there Cooper, like in dead interested."

"Dead is the word guys, dead is the word," said Wunderwear, "believe it. If you want to live find another way. Cooper, my buddy, you have to understand that with Brad stuff comes out of his mouth before stuff goes into his brain."

Cooper pulled Brad away and walked with him up the beach a little. Brad was still protesting, "Hey man, what did I say?"

"If I were you I'd work it out before Isabel reaches thirty six," Cooper chuckled, "luckily you've gotta bit of time."

He left it at that.

Brad wanted to go back and ask Isabel how long but Cooper thought it to be a bad idea.

The family had sunk a few Fosters along the seafront and were walking back to their hotel passing a public toilet when it occurred to them that they were bursting for a piss and that now would be a good time to get some relief.

The toilet was below ground. Brad and Lance gratefully lunged for the gents.

Finished they turned to wash their hands at the basin.

Whoops! Across two sinks was a huge guy, very dark skinned but washing off a large amount of black make up. He turned round and grinned. "Sorry about this mates," he said affably, "but I'm a black fella whose not quite black enough for the tourists so I gotta use make up to look authentic."

"Are you an Abo then?" asked Lance.

"Mostly, but not quite," he answered, "Me Ma was an Aborigine but Pop was a Maori crossed with a Chinese so you can see why I need a bit of authenticity. Pop didn't do well here so went back to NZ. His Pop went back to China. Like all the Chinese labourers he built half the world and then got dumped when surplus to requirements."

"Fucking hell," exclaimed Brad, "so some people had it worse than the Italians and Irish then? Just shows ya dunnit?"

"Yeah," said the Black Fella, "it don't pay to look too hard. Makes you realise why so many believe there's more than one God in the world doesn't it? Too much blame to dump on only one of them. I mean how can you pin all the fuck ups in the world on one God. Only nutcases would do that.

How can you pin all the fuck ups in the world on
just one God? Only nutcases do that!

"Are Catholics nutcases then," asked Brad.

"Nah, of course not," said Lance re-assuringly, "they got three in one and the Devil. Others got at least two like God and Satan. Everyone hedges their bets. Some go for broke and have a God for everything."

"Sounds confusing to me," said Brad.

"Yeah, well welcome to religion," smiled Lance, "the more confusing the better, so they can comfortably fall back on faith. Usually everybody becomes more faithful the older they get. You know the story? Forgive me God, I have been bad at times but I won't be anymore because I'm too bloody old but give me half a chance and I would soon get up to my old tricks. Hey God, will prayer help?"

"Mom would not be happy with you saying that," Brad chuckled, "she prays a lot."

"No wonder with you around," Lance grinned, "you would make Atheists pray because you defy scientific definition. They'd have to turn to something beyond that."

"I take that as a compliment," Brad said smugly, "Wow! I'm beyond scientific definition am I? What a chat up line."

"Anyway," said Lance, turning around, "we're ignoring our friend here. Sorry about that."

"Don't worry, that was just White Fella talk," he said amiably, "been good meeting ya. I'm off to have some tucker. See you around."

"Don't you want your country back," asked Brad, risking a hard look from Lance, "the natives in our country want their land back."

"No need here mate," said the Fella, "lots of space left that no one particularly wants. Not nice for Pink Fellas but we can easy go Walkabout there and around if we want. We just act up Abo and the Pink Fellas go all gooey and patronising. Makes 'em feel all superior. Me, well I'm just me and make a good living working for the tourist board showing people around and explaining what we do and how we do it."

"You are just a fucking old fraud ain't ya," Lance laughed.

"No more than the tourists," answered the Fella, "they walk around with fixed smiles on their faces gawping incredulously at everyday things no matter where they go. Good, ennit? See ya guys."

And he went.

Lance and Brad went back to the others and tried to explain why they took so long but only got as far as telling them that they saw a Black Fella blacking down before they got laughed at for telling tall stories.

They went to a few more bars on the way to eat.

Brad tried out his new chat up technique.

He slid up to the bar alongside two women and waited his chance.

As soon as there was a break in their chatter he jumped in, "hello ladies," he said in what he thought was a smooth talking manner, "how would you like the company of a guy who defies scientific description."

One of the women looked around and said calmly, "love it, where is he? Do you know him?"

Brad didn't blink, "I'm the guy, the very guy, right in front of you. Your lucky day," he said.

The other one looked him up and down," you look more like an alien to me, go back to Mars," she said disdainfully, "fuck off!"

"No, no, what don't you understand," he said frantically, "it is me, it really is me."

"And what don't you understand about fuck off," the woman said pleasantly enough and turned away making it a finality.

Brad was stirred, not shaken and would have kept on trying if Lance hadn't dragged him away, still protesting that it was okay if they thought he was an extraterrestrial. After all they defied scientific description too didn't they?

He quietened down when Lance told him that most descriptions of aliens were negative and they looked like murderous, drivelling lizards.

When this soaked into Brad's skull he wanted to go back and start a war but decided not to when he saw that the women had been joined by three or four very fit young men.

He realised he was hungry after all.

He told Lance in an intense manner, "those dames are not very perceptive. So dim they don't realise they've missed an ideal opportunity to meet the guy of their dreams bro'. What's going wrong with this world?"

"Don't fret man," Lance smiled, "just keep on meeting non perceptive girls and eventually you'll do just fine."

Brad wasn't sure whether that was good advice or not.

He was still sure it was a good line though and was determined to succeed with it.

Fortunately he didn't tell the family.

They all tucked into juicy Australian lamb chops, veggies and baked potato.

Brad of course couldn't resist asking if it was really Skippy they were eating and the waitresses laughed as if they had never heard it before but on their way to the kitchen they raised their eyebrows along with a cynical grimace.

They were imbued with the spirit of keep the customers happy whatever.

Good old OZ!

Buy me a Beer

They had all eaten enough but were sure they hadn't drunk sufficient. After all it was hot and they had to be careful not to dehydrate. A few more beers would do the trick.

"Let's go for a top up," Russ suggested.

He knew of a large bar that featured live blues rock bands. That was enough to start a charge.

It was the size of a small warehouse and almost as basic. The band and sound system were definitely 21st century but the rest was 19th century pub style. Long wooden trestle tables, long wooden benches and sawdust on the floor. A notice proclaimed, "You can't spit but you can vomit!"

They looked around at more signs. "No drugs allowed but overdosing on alcohol permitted!"

"Too much is not enough!"

"Enjoy until oblivion envelopes you!"

"Don't drink and drive - dehydrate instead!"

They decided to sit down and order.

The golden bubbles trapped in long tall glasses were irresistible. They ordered two or three each.

They got stuck into the beers and listened to the band. The volume was high, enough to get the chest vibrating. The thought of vibrating chests got Brad excited and he looked around.

He caught the eye of a contented, handsome lady in her forties. She nodded and came over.

Brad loved it as she definitely fit the bill. She was undeniably his type.

She also had to lean close to him to make herself heard. His heart beat louder than the band's rhythm section.

"How do you like it," she shouted, "everything okay?"

The family started to pay attention.

Brad had lost his voice. Her perfumed hair so near to his face had made him speechless.

"Great place, great band," shouted Lance.

"Yeah," screamed Isabel, "that lead guitar player. He's great. He should go to England. He'd make a fortune."

The woman smiled, "you don't realise what a good thing you've just said. He's my son and he's won a scholarship to the UK. You certainly said the right thing."

She chuckled, "not bad for a Yank and a Pom. They're not usually so bright."

"Isabel grinned, "we try you know, have our moments, but not so sure about him."

She pointed at Brad.

"Yeah," said Lance, "all the time you can't hear him he's just fine."

The woman smiled again, said, "have a good evening," and moved on.

The band took a break.

A character wobbled over to their table. He was lean, gnarled, dressed like a bushman and was drunk.

He also had a snake curled around the brim of his hat.

As he leaned forwards the family leaned back.

With a quick snap of his wrist he whisked the snake off his head and grasped it firmly in one hand. It wriggled and hissed like mad.

"Buy me a beer and you can touch my snake," he garbled.

"Buy me a beer and you can touch my snake," he garbled, waving the reptile around dangerously, "he won't bite you, he's not poisonous. When he gets older he crushes and eats you."

"I don't think that re-assures us," said Isabel hesitantly, "just bugger off will you?"

The character still hung around hopefully.

"Look," said Russ, "we'll buy you a beer if you'll just bugger off like the lady said. We've got a few spares here so take one."

The character wound the snake back around his hat, took a beer in each hand and wandered off without another word.

"Fuck that," exclaimed Brad, "he took two."

Well think yourselves lucky," laughed Cooper, "there's no telling what could happen here. If a guy comes up with a huge croc tucked under his arm then run like fucking hell for the door. Don't offer him a beer."

"Why," asked Brad, "do crocs drink whisky?"

The band started up right then so the family ignored him.

With anyone else it might have been a joke but with Brad you just never knew.

The band took another break.

The character with the snake bounded onto the stage.

"Hello, hello, hello," he said heartedly, "we have in Australia our own native music with its own native instruments. We have the didgeridoos and you are lucky tonight to hear some of them played live."

Three or four aborigines filed onto the stage with instruments of varying sizes. There was one big one the size of an Alpine Horn.

Isabel shouted out, "bloody hell, where's Rolfe Harris?"

"We sent him over and let you keep him in revenge for sending us the Spice Girls and Take That," came the swift answer.

No one laughed. It was after all a serious statement.

The musicians started blowing. The idea was to applaud the fact that they actually managed to get a sound out because what they made was certainly not music. It was reminiscent of the vevuelas that ruined the Football World Cup in South Africa.

They stopped.

"Thank god for that," said Lance, in relief.

"Okay, all right," shouted the character, "now is there anyone in the audience who can show us how it's done. Come on, come up here, get stuck in. Give it a blow!"

"I'm not gonna blow anywhere near him," cried Brad, "the thought makes me shudder."

"So does the action Bro," laughed Lance, "I've seen you and heard you. Isabel and I nearly fell over you and that Thelma on the beach one night.

Thought there was a Tsunami coming in."

"No, no, no, that was no Tsunami coming it was me!" Brad shouted gleefully, "and the Hurricane was Thelma."

"Next time we'll issue a storm warning," said Isabel, "so we can give it a rain check."

The whole family groaned.

But the character was still at it.

He had managed to get four or five likely lads and lasses on the stage.

In any audience there are always a few who are prepared to have a go getting their few minutes of fame even if they look ridiculous.

They always seem to be a mixture of show offs and goofs. You know, white people doing it with great looks of primitive satisfaction. But good on 'em.

First up was a giggling girl.

The character had of course chosen the biggest of all the instruments.

He had to put the girl on a chair before she could reach the mouthpiece.

The character explained that she was used to this as her boyfriend was very tall.

The girl blew hard with puffed out cheeks which soon turned red.

All that came out was a small woof.

Ten times only a small woof.

The character concluded that she had a very frustrated boyfriend unless he had a very small woof.

The rest of the hopefuls managed a few sounds which were loudly applauded. They sounded only a little worse than the pros.

The family were greatly relieved when it was over and the band came back.

"It's funny ennit that the only good music comes from white folk like us," Brad said thoughtfully, "the rest bang or blow a load of old junk don't they? Not music is it? Just tuneless like the sounds kids make."

"Do you like this band and what they play buddy?" asked Lance.

"Of course, great ain't it?" Brad smirked, "white band ain't it?"

"Black music," said Lance.

"What?" exclaimed Brad.

"Jazz, blues, rock and roll and gospel come from the African mix in America," said Lance, "I tell ya you've never heard anything as spine chilling as the harmonies that come out of Africa. Makes a barber shop quartet sound tame. Good but tame. And those middle eastern rhythms really get you moving.

You've gotta get your head out of your mp3 and listen around more."

Brad seemed puzzled. "Geez, so it comes from everywhere," he said, "well at least West of China and Thailand. No wonder they loved rock and roll there, with all that weird screechy stuff they had goin' on!"

They all walked back to the hotel singing "That 'ole time rock an' roll."

Sort of in time and more or less in tune.

Sparring Partners

They moved on to Sydney.

They did the lot. Dinner at the Rocks, round harbour boat trip, cross the bridge, tour of the Opera House and Bondi Beach. Found a couple of Greek restaurants on Pitt Street.

Cooper turned up one morning with a pickup truck. They all bundled in and on. Of they went into the bush.

The treat was a Kangaroo and Ostrich farm.

The ostriches weren't farmed for their meat. They were farmed for racing.

The family were amazed at the speed. Those Ostriches really flew along.

"What do you do with them when they are too old to race?" asked Lance, "do you eat them or what?"

"Nah, old Ostrich tastes rubbish," said one of the hands, "wouldn't even repair old boots with it. We slaughter them and grind it all up for animal feed. Tasty, the beasts love it."

Jeanette looked horrified.

"Don't believe him, he's just winding you up," said another, "they're used for taming and training and then retired. Not much good with arthritis and osteoporosis are they? Just like my Gran."

"God you're all wind up artists aren't you," said Cooper, "let's go and see Skippy."

"Aha," said one guy, "Mike Tyson is up for a scrap today. Ready to take on all comers."

"Mike Tyson? Here?" asked Isabel, "really?"

"Yep, really, he's our champ. Our very own Kangaroo Killer Diller. He'll whack you one but he won't bite your ear off. Well he's not done that so far. Anyone fancy their chances?"

No one moved.

"Come on. Anyone?"

No one moved.

"You poor lot. None of you want to take on an old kangaroo past his prime?"

Suddenly there was a bit of a shuffle forwards.

Brad was on the move looking daggers over his shoulder as Lance and Cooper shoved him forwards.

"Nah, nah," he said anxiously, "not that I'm scared or that but I don't want to hurt some old guy even if he fancies himself as Mike Tyson."

"It's not a guy Brad, it's a kangaroo," Lance explained carefully, "you know, the bouncy, bouncy kind who carry their kids in a pouch bag."

"That's it then. Its definitely not for me. That's cruelty to dumb animals that is," Brad cried in relief.

"It's all right, we won't let him hurt you very much," said the guy, actually putting into words the thoughts of the others. "Which one was the dumb animal?"

Brad couldn't get out of it.

His hands were bandaged, a pair of silk shorts were found to fit him, boots and gloves were laced up and a flashy dressing gown draped round his shoulders.

He looked in the mirror and ran for it.

When they finally caught up with him he agreed to take part if he could wear his normal clothes including baseball cap.

Everyone agreed on the basis that it would be easier to distinguish which one was the animal.

Just when Brad was feeling a bit better about it one of the promotors decided to be helpful.

"Don't worry too much," he said, "if you get hurt we have first class medical facilities here. It's all about sports. We even have acupuncture, we believe that can cure anything and anyone."

"Oh yeah," laughed Isabel," for god's sake don't try it on a haemophiliac then. Bad idea."

The guy looked puzzled and then took out his ipad and looked it up on Wickiepedia. After reading for a few minutes he looked even more puzzled.

"Yeah matey," chuckled Isabel, "you be careful who you stick pins in and also where you stick'em."

"Why do they want to stick pins in me," Brad said plaintively, "is it voodoo or something?"

"Close enough," said Isabel, "now get going or we'll all throw darts at you."

Brad and the kangaroo were led into a roped off ring. Smaller than normal but big enough for Brad to prance around bouncing off the ropes hurling his hands up in the air and then frantically shadow boxing in his corner.

The kangaroo didn't move a muscle and showed complete lack of interest.

The referee went to each corner and explained the rules.

The bell sounded and Brad came out cagily from his corner, guard up and head tucked down.

The kangaroo took no notice.

Brad went closer, touched the gloves and then tried a few speculative jabs.

The kangaroo didn't move.

Brad stopped, looked quizzically around, dangled his arms limply by his side, and raised his eyebrows in a what do I do now expression.

Big mistake.

Skippy came to life and showed his Killer Diller side.

He bounced forward and delivered a short hard jab landing square on Brad's unprotected chin.

The kangaroo was up but Brad was down. Somehow his baseball cap stayed on.

Skippy now was bouncing around all over the ring, gloves flailing the air as though fighting an army. Brad tried to struggle to his feet but as soon as he moved the kangaroo jumped on him, flapping his long feet all over Brad's body.

"Fuckin' 'ell," he shouted, "I'm gonna kill this fuckin' animal when I get up. It's out of control."

The bell went for the end of the round.

A second came and led the kangaroo back to its corner.

Brad had to find his own way back. With difficulty.

Lance and Cooper sat him down, tried to shut up his protests and failed.

They sponged his face and then tipped the bucket of water over him.

Brad was spluttering, "what's the matter with you, its over. Didn't you hear the bell?"

"Yes, of course we did, that's why we're working on you. That was only the first round."

"Whaaaat," shouted Brad, "how many fucking rounds are there for Christ's sake?"

"Three," said Lance, as he pulled Brad to his feet and shoved him out to the middle of the ring as the bell went.

Brad glanced back over his shoulder to look at Cooper and Lance with daggers in his eyes.

Big mistake. They gestured at him to turn round and as he did so Killer Diller socked him flat on the jaw again. Brad went down poleaxed and then crawled over to his corner and threw in the towel. Fight over.

The kangaroo was definitely up for it.

Brad was definitely down and out of it.

The family expressed their disappointment at Brad's performance but nobody volunteered to take his place and show how it should be done.

Isabel reckoned she had seen more life in a tramps vest and Cooper reckoned that he had seen more excitement at an Undertakers convention.

Russ chuckled, "yep, if they were entertaining their customers they would have been dead boring, wouldn't they?"

After that one the family decided that they needed some refreshment and drove to the nearest bar.

Aussie Rules

They settled down with a huge jug full of beer, golden bubbles. They were thirsty so the first glasses went down quickly, followed by two more.

The booze went straight through Brad.

"Where's the bathroom," he asked urgently.

"Bathroom?" asked Cooper, "what the bloody hell do you need with a bathroom? Shower later in the hotel. You can't do it here. You'll get bloody arrested"

"For crissakes I cant wait that long, I'm bursting," Brad managed to gasp.

"He wants to piss," explained Lance.

"Why not say so? He needs the toilet right?," exclaimed Cooper, "what's with this bathroom stuff? Don't tell me you Americans urinate and crap in the bath. There's more than a slight difference between a toilet basin and a bath. You Yanks worry me at times."

"Worry you!" cried Wunderwear, "they bloody well terrify me. They throw an egg around and call it football and football they call soccer. Some American professor has dreamed up some pathetic reasons for this which don't make sense as usual. Some idiots even quote him. He says that soccer comes from shortening the phrase association football. Maybe but you don't hear anyone saying association soccer do you. It's the FA, not SA, It's FIFA, not SIFA, it's UEFA, not UESA, it's Fussball not Soccerball, its Futbol, not Soccerbol and so on forever. Wake up Yanks, get in line! And as for our language, they've destroyed it by too much fucking swearing!"

"Oh no! Not this again," shouted Brad, "I can't hold on. I'm going," and he rushed off following the signs for the toilet.

He only got as far as the end of the bar before a hand was stuck out stopping him dead in his tracks.

Behind the hand was a huge arm and and attached to the arm was a huge body.

Brad turned to face a rough, tough looking guy. The guy looked intense and serious.

"Hold on there a minute mate," he said, "what's the hurry? Stop right there a second." He turned and grinned at a couple of friends who looked just as rough and tough as him.

Brad thought, "oh hell, this is not a good moment. I don't want any trouble here at any time but right now with a bladder about to burst then this is my Armageddon."

Before wondering how he thought up such a big word out of nowhere he just managed to gasp, "what's up?"

"What's up?" laughed the guy to his pals, "what's up he says?"

They all laughed dutifully. Brad didn't.

slow down mate, we come from Darwin, up there
we shoot anything that goes that fast!

"I'll tell you what's up," chuckled the guy, "We come from Darwin. Up there we shoot anything that moves that fast. Slow down mate and have a beer."

Brad gratefully told them to get one in for him and then shot into the toilet.

When he came out his new friends patted him on the back and told him what a good sport he was. The family looked on in amazement.

The family didn't know quite what to do. Did Brad need rescuing or what?

No worries. Brad brought his Darwin drinking pals over to meet them seemingly a little uncomfortable.

Perhaps there were worries!

"Howdya do," said the Darwinites very politely. "pleased to meet ya."

"Understand from my mate Brad here that you're a mixed bunch, sort a group a mongrels like," one of them said in a friendly enough tone, "some Yanks, Poms and Aussies. We get all sorts down 'ere but we try to keep independent. None of this political correctness malarky. You know telling people exactly what to think without thinking. We lot, well we practice abstinence in moderation."

"Yeah," grinned another, "you see him there? Well he's the intellectual type. You know the kind who reads books instead of watching a porno movie. He even goes to the library when it ain't raining."

They all nudged each other, full of themselves and friendship, working on making an impression.

"We work hard we do. Don't need nothing from no one. We stand on our own two feet."

Wunderwear couldn't help herself, "yeah but you didn't make the shoes and socks that's on them did you?

Silence.

Then.

"You're the Pom?"

"Yes," Wunderwear answered proudly.

"Typical. Can't make your mind up whether you wanna be in Europe or the Commonwealth can you?" stated one of the guys, "We reckon you need Europe more but keep the Commonwealth so that right old useless political bastards can get in on a photo shoot feeling important from time to time."

"The flag guys, don't forget the flag. Seeing the Union Jack flying around helps them still believe in Empire."

"Yep, and it means there are a lot of places you can send your unemployed Royals to to make them feel useful," said another, "the old lady, the Queen's okay, but why did she have those kids of hers?"

"That's just it," said the first, "she has to have kids and they have to have kids. That's her job. She has to keep the line going."

"Don't we all, don't we all do that?"

"Yes but we don't have to do it, do we? We've got a choice, she hasn't. She's gotta do it even if she doesn't fancy it. That's why they give her a palace."

"You mean the Royals have to do it as part of their job? No wonder they walk around with their noses in the air, trying to look all superior."

"Don't know why they think they're superior. They are probably turning their noses up at having to do it. Those who do it they reward and give titles to. Anyway don't we have names for people who do it as a job?"

"Doesn't matter now does it? The princes in history always had mistresses. Gave 'em titles as a reward for opening their legs for the royal cock, but they never married one of them did they? Now we got one who did! Bad news. Just imagine Queen Nell Gwynn. Queen of the whores."

"I can," one chuckled, "her oranges had the royal seal of approval, they would really have been her crowning glory."

"Listen, don't miss the point. We're talking about women here getting out of hand. Look mateys in this world the strong survive. Stags,

Rams, Bulls and all the rest of the male population lock horns in deadly battle," said one drunken, earnest man, "not for sport but for shagging rights over lots of females. Yeah! Fruity mate. We've lost the way. Gotta get back to route one.

I mean chickens lay eggs, we can eat everything from them, they're useful. Where are women useful, what do they lay? Out of action for a week every month and bitchy in between. Animals are useful, we need to copy the animals a lot more. We need to reduce the number of weaker men by warfare. There the strong survive and can get stuck into the women. Tell ya, they'll love it. They don't wanna admit it but they'd love it."

"Wait a minute, you don't have to copy animals, you are animals. Evolution missed you lot out." cried Wunderwear, "don't you guys ever stop? I reckon you should be entertainers."

"Do you reckon? Wow, what shall we do? Where would we perform?" they cried.

"A zoo," replied Wunderwear, "we would put in you as rangers in a safari park. The animals would be terrorists. You deserve each other. We would give you Humvees and the tourists would have Hummers. We would have notices saying ~ Do not get out of your Hummer unless attacked by IEDS."

"Jesus, you are nuts," said one of the men, "what about safety?"

"Easy," replied Wunderwear, "it would be virtual reality, because you guys are unreal. You don't know much about modern war either. The strong don't lead and win in battle anymore with the weaker dying first in hand to hand combat. Some male prick evened up the score with explosives, weapons and aircraft. The strong die first up front, the brainy ones, the weaker, are behind controlling everything. They survive. Remember the meek shall inherit the earth. And as for the EU, well for your information the British would be more enthusiastic if it wasn't so full of foreigners."

"Good day Gentlemen, nice to see you."

"Yep," said Lance, "all wars are hell but losing one is worse."

The family retired gracefully.

They didn't go very far. Only to the next bar.

On the way they had to avoid several people texting and talking on their handphones and jumped for their lives with drivers wandering about in the road punching in an sms. Crazy.

Jeanette looked at Mom who appeared angry and horrified.

"Don't worry Mom, you are old enough to remember when people were observant and looked around them intelligently not acting like robotic morons all the time looking down. We are used to it. A really bright guy would invent human radar. No need to use your eyes."

"Nah," smirked Brad, "the opticians would rebel. No need for specs. Don't forget as soon as something new comes out someone will straight away be against it. Groucho Marx once sang something like - if there's something in it then I'm agin it, I'm agin it, I'm agin it! That was years ago and nothing's changed. You know, deliberately obtuse, trying to be smartasses. They can always claim, ~ God on my side."

"Too right. Okay, let's avoid those who have no idea what's going on around them and dodge in here," said Lance pointing to a garish bar just in front of them, "we're participators not just voyeurs.

They were in Pitt Street, looking up at the peculiar monorail that ate chunks out of the corner of buildings as it wound it's way down to Darling Harbour.

Practical but imperfect.

Wunderwear hoped they wouldn't attract any attention as no matter where she was she seemed to have a flashing light on her head with a sign that said ~ nutcases apply here.

She hoped this would be different.

It wasn't!

They were relaxing when a fella looking so much like a secondhand car salesman came over to them.

They resisted the temptation to run so settled instead for sitting tight and studiously avoided looking at him.

It didn't work.

"Hello good people," a voice said coming out from underneath a rather old fashioned pork pie hat.

"Does anyone still wear something like that," Isabel thought.

Apparently so.

Nobody paid any attention to him.

He tried again, "hello good people, don't ignore me please. Be friendly, respect me."

Lance broke the silence for the family, "Listen pal, whenever someone says to me ~ respect me ~ then they always want something from me, they have nothing to give. So no thank you and goodbye."

"Ah I can tell from your accents that you are visitors to this great country of ours. Welcome," said the Hat, "you look prosperous so how about a little investment here. How about some property. I got some real good bargains."

"I'm sure you have," said Russ, "but I'm Australian, born and bred and don't need any help in looking for a house thank you. My wife is American and these are our families. We're touring at the moment. My family is staying but the rest will go home eventually. Need I say more?"

"No, no of course not, it's good to go home," he said hastily, "there are too many coming here anyway. The wrong sort you know. The ones leaving everything behind them and bringing nothing with them. They pay a fortune to get here on dodgy boats and then tell us they've got nothing left and expect us to clothe, shelter and feed them. Why have we got to do it? Why can't their governments do it? Their politicians and cronies drive around in flashy cars between four or five mansions, all in their wive's and families' names of course, living off the generous foreign aid payments supposed to help their people who actually never see any of it."

"That's precisely why they come, dumbo," chuckled Isabel, "they don't see any of it. Get it now? Their governments push them down, they don't build them up. If they try to get up then they get smashed down. Their armies fight for the corrupt, not their country. So they come for a chance for freedom, security under the law and a better life. Of course you can't take them all, that's also unreal but don't slag off people who've already suffered enough humiliation to last several lifetimes. They don't give all their savings, leave everything behind, bring their families across hundreds of miles of dangerous oceans in sinking boats risking their lives just for welfare. You can't give all but a little from you could be a lot to them. You don't have to make it too easy but you don't have to make it impossible either. Give people hope."

"All very nice and comfy to talk high and mighty like that but there are many who agree with me and write articles criticising your benevolence. Important people," he smirked, "I mean if muslims mean well why do they always ask if you are moslem. I don't ask, you don't ask. Why do they?"

"Earlier you were interested in our nationality, why can't they be interested in religion?" answered Isabel, "anyways there's always somebody somewhere willing to pay someone to say something nice about something bad. Always someone to make excuses for the inexcusable and to take payment for it. Whose paying you?"

"Oh if you are going to shout and talk to me like that then I won't discuss this any further. Fancy screaming at me like that," he said pathetically.

"Screaming," laughed Isabel, "no one screamed. Only you like a stuck pig. Who's gone all weak and feeble now? Where's the strong macho male hunter? Can't take a little retaliation huh? We've seen it all before. So cocky until challenged. Get out of here you wimp. You're the type who's only good with a gun in his hands against unarmed opposition."

He hesitated, looked about to say a lot more but maybe saw a little of Wunderwear Woman appearing. He decided against staying.

The words of Isabel followed him out.

"This country was invaded by immigrants years ago. They were prisoners and their gaolers from Britain. I can easily guess which lot you came from, obviously the gaolers."

She paused and then threw in, "I bet when you dress up you wear your good shirt outside your trousers."

"Isabel, what's this about the shirt?" asked Lance.

"Well originally the kids started a young fashion by wearing proper shirts outside their trousers as a sort of kids rebellion against the adults. You know, 'tuck your shirts in properly', so they didn't. They were horrified when their dads copied and did it too. So they stopped. They realised what a lot of wallies they looked. Unfortunately the adults didn't, so some idiots still carry on thinking it makes them look young and trendy. It doesn't. Get it?"

" Okay, I got it," smiled Lance, "thank god I haven't done that for ages, let's move on?"

"There are too many coming here, you know, mainly the wrong sort."

State of the Union

They did move on. Shopping. As always great for the girls, boring for the boys. They had all piled into Cooper's truck, some inside, some out.

Russ was driving and looking for a carpark space.

Isabel looked at him enquiringly.

"Nothing for us as usual," Russ moaned, "no parking spots."

"What about all those spaces over there, and look at that one there, perfect?" she said, "can't believe you didn't see 'em."

"Yeah, what marvellous eyesight you got," he smirked, "course I can see 'em. But they're not for us are they?"

"Who the bloody hell are they for then," Isabel cried, eyebrows raised to the roof.

"These two here are for disabled and all those others are for ladies," he explained patiently, "that's a lady's only parking zone."

"Who thought that one up?" Isabel sniggered, "what's all that for?"

"Safety," said Russ, "there's been a coupla muggings so the bigwigs thought they should put all the women together."

Isabel roared out loud, "typical bookworm thinking. Let's stop the muggers by helping them. Put all the women in one place so they can find 'em easily. Bulk, off the shelf, instant mugging facilities. Who cares about men and families anyway. Let's leave all of them in the previous danger zone."

"Yeah, right on," Brad said, leaning over from the back seat, "we men are the latest endangered species. Women get all the protection, tell the most unbelievable stories, continually murmur the word ~ abuse ~ and stand back waiting for the usual gasps of horror. They cry ~ pms ~ and then murder us. You smile at them and they claim harassment, you don't smile at them and they claim you seemed threatening. They drink too much, take too many drugs, get carried away by mad sex and then claim date rape. You have a relationship that they break up and they get most of what you've got and as for kissing with tongues, well, you're dead and gone man."

He took a deep breath.

"Have you quite finished," asked Isabel, "It seems to have escaped you that I wasn't necessarily serious. I was being less than subtly sarcastic."

"Well if I was you I'd take something for it," said Brad, "it's very misleading. I was confused and still am."

Yep, about normal," laughed Jeanette, "go and try some tongues bro."

Russ suddenly shot forwards watching a nearby family intently.

They were walking about, bewildered, looking for their car. One pointed and went one way while another pointed and went another. The remainder kept turning round and round looking utterly lost.

"Make your bloody minds up for crissakes. We need your space. You obviously didn't use your phones to take a photo, did you? Easy that 'ennit? For fucks sake try your remote," he shouted.

They couldn't hear him but they did pump the remote and suddenly they were all smiles. They'd found it.

Russ shadowed them.

They were nervous at that, looking anxiously over their shoulders and muttering, but they kept going. It slowly dawned on them what was happening and they relaxed and became over helpful, slowing down pointing the way.

"Oh for god's sake just get in and get going," snarled Russ through a fixed grin.

Eventually, after much dispute over who was sitting where, they did.

As soon as they pulled out, he pulled in.

"Right" said Lance, "let's get this straight. Gals to the shops, boys to the bar. Okay?"

That's what they did.

After four or five rounds the boys didn't care about the time. If the girls wanted to shop longer then that was fine. Just get some more beers in.

Eventually the girls turned up, shopping saturated.

Cooper and Russ were huddled together, whispering and chuckling.

"All right, what's going on," asked Jeanette authoritatively, with a cement like smile on her face, "no secrets. Why the conspiracy."

"Well we are from Brisbane," Russ said defiantly, emphasizing each word as though that settled everything.

"Yeah, so?" asked Jeanette, even more authoritatively.

"Well we're in Sydney, ain't we?" replied Russ, spreading out his hands in an expansive gesture. He looked around furtively.

"Okay," said Jeanette, "fuck the geography lesson, I know where we are and where we're not, even without global GPS. What's the point?"

"State of the Union 'ennit," blurted out Cooper, looking at them all as though they were dumb.

"So your President is going to deliver an address on the state of the country," said Lance, "big deal, we have to listen to that crap all the time, but we don't crouch down out of sight whispering, do we?"

"Feel like it at times though, listening to all that bullshit," grumbled Mom.

"Nah, nah, nah, not that" laughed Russ, "it's rugby. Well sort of. More like war actually. New South Wales against Queensland."

"They're two of the states in Australia," added Cooper helpfully.

"So what about the other states?" asked Isabel.

"They don't count," laughed Russ, "Rugby's a man's game."

"Now I know why you were secretive," grinned Lance, "is it that serious?"

The girls turned up - shopping saturated!

"Bloody hell mate, it's worse than that," exclaimed Cooper, "it's close to annihilation and that's just the fans. You would not wanna be on the pitch."

"I can understand it a bit you know," Isabel said nodding her head sagely, "I was in Ireland when their team had a World Cup run under a Geordie manager called Jackie Charlton. In a pub I was having a drink. I only had English pound notes, no Irish punds and I asked the barman if it was okay. He asked me what I was drinking and of course I said Guinness. He told me that if it was Guinness I was drinking then he would take the worthless English paper." She smiled at the memory.

"Yeah, so?" asked Cooper, a little mystified, "what's that to do with all this?"

"Oh yeah right," laughed Isabel, "well you see there was a right old ruckus going on in another bar."

"Yeah, okay," said Russ, "we're holding our breath girl."

"I asked the barman what was going on," replied Isabel, "and he said the match had just started, you know, the international? Forgot who they were playing now but I asked if I could join in and watch. Well the guy asked me in all seriousness whether I wanted to watch it in the lounge in a civilised way or did I want to join the animals in the bar. If I went in with the animals then I would be locked in for the duration. We would of course be fed and watered. I went in with the animals. I was very young at the time. A backpacking student."

Silence.

"Is that it?" Cooper said flatly, "there was no riot, you weren't raped or anything?"

"No, of course not, they were a noisy lot but fun and they were gentlemen," Isabel said indignantly.

"Then things have bloody well changed a lot since they came here," laughed Russ, "what the hell happened to the 'Wild Rover'? That's what comes of joining the EU. You all become as boring as the Germans and as moody as the French."

"Make good cars though," Brad said thoughtfully.

"Who," asked Russ, "the French?"

"No," replied Brad, "the Germans. Wish I could afford one."

"Easy, chuckled Isabel, "just go and become a politician's crony in an underdeveloped country. Got tons of 'em there. The Germans even boast about the sales in their emerging markets. Good job they don't ask where the money comes from."

"But they never do, do they?" asked Mom, entering the conversation, "all this so called caring stuff is so superficial, just barely skin deep. The ones who really care are out there doing something about it. They don't get glamorous photographic shoots, patting each other on the back, do they, pretending they know it all? They're there all the time. Heroes if you ask me."

"Go for it Mom," shouted Brad, "go get 'em."

"As for the media butterflies - well. Just headliners. Drop in, drop out and then drop it for good," she exclaimed, warming to her subject, "they find all these weird experts, all smug ain't they, when they really need a darn good shaking up and as for the questions asked by the anchormen ---"

"Anchor person Mom," Lance interrupted, "anchor persons. You can't say anchormen, it's sexist."

"That's what I mean, that's what's wrong. No one knows who they are anymore. No one knows if they're supposed to be men or women," she cried, "give us your impressions of the mood where you are, they ask, what's happening on the ground? or bring us up to date on what's the latest, and so on. All this when the network has just spent a while showing dead bodies and damage all over the place, giving some background here and there, usually repeating the same pictures over and over again. You don't need some reporter dressed in flack jacket and helmet to tell you that the locals are angry, pissed off and bloody bewildered, do you?"

"It looks like to me that we've come back to the rugby again," Russ laughed, "interviewing the losers. Dangerous."

"Oh no we haven't," Mom exclaimed, "I've not finished yet. I've not talked about the boring Northern Europeans, you know, Germans, English the like.

I won't talk about them because they are boring. Not like us Latins. We love our big nobs to be involved in scandal. They're human. Not hypercritical pre programmed robots. The northerners need to get a life. Work, work, work, as though that's all there is. Worship the god of efficiency. They remind me of the mice in the spinning wheel. No matter how fast they go they never really get anywhere. Never get ahead of themselves. What's the point?"

Everyone was quiet for a moment, then -----.

"Make good cars though, how do I get to be a corrupt crony in a developing country?" Brad mused, "sounds okay to me!"

"It seems Sydney is not a good influence on Brad's thinking," Cooper grinned, glancing around at everyone.

"When we find a place that is then we'll leave him there," said Jeanette without humour.

"Oh boy, I reckon we done enough here, let's go back up north and enjoy ourselves," said Russ.

The Borders

After relaxing a day on the Gold Coast, Russ suggested a drive out.

They drove down to an old river border crossing between Queensland and New South Wales. There was a large pub besides the river. There was no bridge. The river was narrow and shallow so could be easily forded.

Russ explained that it was here that the sheepmen crossed with their herds in the old days, watering the sheep and themselves before going on to the market. They all rode horseback and used sheep dogs. Those who were old and crotchety came in horse drawn buggies.

"I have a question," Brad interrupted with a sloppy grin on his face.

"Yeah mate, wadya wanna know," said Cooper co-operatively.

"Well in Sheepdog trials," he said, "who do they find guilty? The sheep or the dogs?" He smiled as though he had just had a great philosophical moment.

They all groaned.

"Take no notice," said Jeanette mournfully, "he spouts absolute rubbish with the utmost conviction. If he went to a mind reader he would be given a discount."

"He should be a politician then, or a diplomat," laughed Mom, "or more likely a Republican."

"Listen," Isabel said earnestly, "when he went on a parachute course he got worried and confused. Suddenly woke up that it was dangerous. He didn't last long."

"No," cried Jeanette, laughing her head off, "He didn't want a reserve chute. He demanded an airbag that opened on impact. He wanted a guaranteed soft landing."

"Anyway," Russ continued doggedly, in spite of the interruptions, "the sheepmen laughed and sang, gambled and fought, totally happy unless the beer ran out. To drink a bar dry was a great achievement for the drinkers but a disgrace for the pub owner. The resulting behaviour from punters queueing up for a drink and being disappointed was never good. At best some damage could be expected. At worst there could be total destruction."

"Yeah, okay, got that," said Mom, "but how did they get to market if they were either beat up, dead drunk or just dead?"

"Easy," said Cooper, "the horses took 'em. As long as they could sit a horse or collapse in a buggy the horses ambled on to where ever they needed to go. The dogs did the rest. Nobody got charged for being drunk in charge of a horse, a dog or a buggy. Those were the days."

"Well we've come a long way since then," said Russ's Mum, "progress and all that ya know."

"Progress," roared Isabel, "we've gone nowhere. Some nutcases are developing robots like mad and now they've got a computer controlled car that drives itself. We can soon get blind drunk, be carried home by a robot or taken back by a self-driven car. Me, I prefer the horse. Much safer and more intelligent than a bloody computer."

"That's true actually," said Cooper, "if a guy gets lost in the outback, needs water and doesn't stupidly take over thinking he knows better than his horse then the beast will always find it before he does. If he trusts the horse he might get sorted and live."

"If he trusts his handphone and gps then he might get sorted even quicker," smiled Lance, "now that's progress. How about trying to drink this place dry?"

They didn't succeed but gave it a good go all the same.

After a while they noticed that Brad was looking downcast and morose.

He wasn't joining in the fun and games. Frankly they weren't nearly as funny and witty as they thought themselves to be but they were at least making an attempt at projecting happiness. The booze helped as always.

The family exchanged glances, raised eyebrows and pulled faces.

Brad didn't notice, or at least he pretended he didn't.

"Okay Bro' what's with you then?" Lance asked at last, "what's on your mind man?"

"Oh, so at least you think I might have one then," Brad replied dully, still looking down at his beer.

"Do what!?" Lance exclaimed, "what you on about?"

"My mind. All I get are snide remarks. Ridicule," moaned Brad soulfully, "none of you can see I'm being deliberately off the wall at times, can you? Beyond you, ain't it, that your bro can be hurt by your very, oh so very funny putdowns? Too much effort to see that I am saying and doing some things on purpose merely to lighten up. Sometimes I wonder just who the dumb clucks are in this family."

"Whoops," cried Isabel, "seems apologies are necessary. I'm sure I speak for everyone here when I say we are sorry if our insensible remarks offended you in any way."

"Yeah well, alright then," Brad smiled at last, "from now on please take notice that I'm a bit of an intellectual. You have a genius in your midst."

"Right genius," laughed Mom, "what great utterances have you got for us today?"

"'erm, well, 'er nothing immediately," Brad said hesitantly.

"Oh come on, there must be something going on in your brain you want to share with us," said Jeanette encouragingly.

"Right, well there was something that came to me the other day. Sort of enlightening like," Brad said humbly, "do you want to hear it?"

"Can't wait," laughed Lance, "go on."

"Ya see, in school we all learnt that heat expanded things, didn't we, right? and that cold contracted things?" Brad explained laboriously.

"Right again," said Lance, "is there a point to this?"

"Yep, of course," exclaimed Brad triumphantly, "simple, heat makes longer, cold makes shorter see? So that is why the days are longer in summer and shorter in winter."

Brad mistook the stunned silence for admiration.

"Also, wait for it, I got another," he said joyfully, apparently loving the moment, "I can't help these things happening in my head. I bet you don't know the real reason they build all the airports well out of town do you"

No one dared answer. They all waited for the revelation. For sure they felt it would be original. They were not disappointed.

"Well it makes sense to put the buildings where the aeroplanes go dunnit? I mean they put the railway stations where the trains go don't they? They put gas stations where the cars go and shops where the shoppers go. So they put airports where the planes go," he said intently, "see it now? I didn't get it before but got it now. It's obvious once you make the connection. I often make break throughs like that. When you have a mind like mine then such things are simple ain't they?"

At first there was a long silence as the family pretended to absorb what had been said. They struggled but managed to just about keep straight faces.

Everyone present nodded sagely before replying in unison, "yes, we reckon simple is exactly the right word for it."

Brad smiled, totally mollified, and joined in the subsequent final outburst of hilarity.

He felt enveloped in total family love.

Benefits

As with everyone everywhere the conversation and jokes slowly tailed off and as always there came a time when the other people in the bar slowly came into focus. They had run out of absent friends to laugh about and sneer at so took in their surroundings and occupants.

No one anywhere at first glance matched up meriting their wit and attention. No glamour. Only dowdy and boring.

However.

Close to them was a small noisy group. The family had been so rowdy and wrapt up in themselves that they hadn't noticed their neighbours before.

Isabel perked up. They had strident London accents. She and the others zoomed up and tuned in.

"Bloody 'ell, I 'adn't thought being pregnant could be so uncomfortable," a frumpy, lumpy looking girl said, slumped back in a chair.

"Well it's never gonna be a bed of roses gel is it?" said an older woman with horn rimmed glasses and bouffant hair set in cement, "when I carried you it was blue bloody murder. Sick I was for months and I thought you was gonna be a bleedin footballer the way you was kicking. After you was born you never stopped moaning or moving. Been the same ever since."

"Oh for crissakes, you've bin singin' that song for years. Thought you'd 'ave got over it by now," groaned lumpy, "I'm bloody well nearly thirty, 'en I?"

"Yeah, and not acting a day bloody older than the day I 'ad yer," Cement Hair said accusingly, "I don't suppose you've worked out who the father is 'ave ya? A bit difficult that one is ennit?"

"Ah nah nah, don't get carried away," Lumpy sneered, "I've worked it back ain't I? It was in Thailand wan' it? It wasn't the little Asian pimp, he was so small he slipped out before we got going. I tried to pull 'im back in but he took 'is chance and run for it. It was probably the big bald German who kept asking how it was for me. He was pumping and thumping so hard I was too out of breath to answer. When he came he nearly broke his back and mine too. 'E was singing bleeding Deutschland uber Alles most of the time even when I was uber 'im."

"Mind you it could have been the backpacking addict. He was so stoned he tried to fuck the cuddly bear on my pillow. Gave a new meaning to a good stuffing. When I finally got him to deliver the goods in the right place he said I was Eve and he was giving me the serpent from Paradise. His dick was so short, red and round I thought it was more like the apple."

"Yeah, really helpful that, ennit? Bloody memories," laughed Cement Hair, "what about work, what about where to live, what about support when we get 'ome? Don't come to me."

"Don't come to me either," an anaemic looking bloke chipped in from behind them, "nothing to do with me. I'm just an ex partner who came along for the ride and got dumped."

"Lucky bloody you then, ennit?" chuckled Cement Hair, "just imagine trying to bring up a stoned backpacking kid who might 'ave a Kraut accent fertilised in Thailand. What's it gonna do, apply for an EU immigrant visa."

"Yeah, go on and enjoy yourselves a bit while ya can," Lumpy cried, "I'll be alright won' I when we get 'ome? They gotta give me long leave with pay ain't they? They gotta get me an 'ouse to live in. They gotta give me pay and allowances ain't they? Can't sack me can they? That's sexual discrimination ain't it? I mean why should I pay for one little slip up? Let them pay, they got the dough."

Isabel had gradually been morphing into Wunderwear Woman the longer the conversation went on.

"Oi you! Who is the they?" she exploded, "I and every other responsible person is the they. We ordinary folk are the they. We are the they who have to pay for the morons like you and your one little slip. One little slip up be buggered you tart. Take the bloody responsibility yourself you selfish pratt."

The trio first looked stunned, then offended, then mad.

"Who the bloody 'ell asked you to butt in," shouted Cement Hair.

"Yeah, if we wanted your bleedin' opinion we would 'ave asked for it, wouldn't we?" said Anaemic looking about as threatening as a wet lettuce, his nobbly knees almost knocking together.

"Oi you, Mr. Ex, keep your fucking nose out of this," snarled Lumpy, looking daggers at him.

Anaemic backed off obviously deeply hurt with an offended air all about him. Nobody noticed.

"We didn't come all the way on holiday to Australia just to get insulted by a fucking upper class English Fascist re-actionary," Lumpy bawled very loudly, "let's get out of 'ere?"

"Yep," laughed Wunderwear, "go back to the UK. If you get insulted there you can act offended and play the victim. You didn't have to come so far. Why spend so much when you could have got pissed on the benefit money back in the local pub. God help the baby with you lot around."

"Humpff," snorted Cement Hair, "people like you will never understand the likes of us, so bugger off and mind ya own business."

The trio left in a huff shrugging their shoulders irritably.

"Oh boy, you really handled that well," Lance grinned, "persuaded them to change didn't you? They'll go back and work for a living after that won't they?"

"Nah, never change them, born scroungers and layabouts they are," said Wunderwear, "problem is that they give such a bad impression that ordinary people begrudge the help being given to people who really need it and there are plenty of them."

Lumpy, Cement Hair and Anaemic celebrate ripping off the system.

"There are many more who are deserving and don't shake down the system but you don't hear so much from them and about them do you? So many people just don't think," Russ's Mum said simply. "I reckon it's all due to there being too many people in the world," she chuckled, "too many bodies and not enough brains to go round."

Pop, her husband joined in, "I'm always fascinated by the people who tell others to get a life but never seem to have one themselves. I see these young girls excitedly saying they're wild which means they wear short skirts showing their bums and wear tops that that show their bellies and boobs and get drunk and sloppy. That's wild? Huh, they don't do anything that nobody else can't do."

"Yeah, Pops, can just see you showing your bum and boobs, that would be wild all right," cried Cooper, laughing his head off, "is that what you do to turn Mum on?"

"Not funny son, not funny. I meant doing something really exciting for a change. Ask Mum, showing my bum and boobs might get me arrested but it won't give anyone a thrill."

"I have a nephew who might like it though," Mom chuckled, "never seen him to be very fussy. Want to try it out?"

"Give that one a pass, thank you," Pop said decisively, "change the subject please."

"Okay but that girl screwed around, took chances with unprotected sex, fucked strangers and then saw nothing wrong with the government having to sweep up her crap afterwards," said Jeanette looking concerned, "I'm no saint but I had too much respect and dignity to behave like that. She makes whores look decent. They don't pay tax but they don't ask the state to pay for them either, do they?"

"Nope," smiled Brad, "whores will never support DIY either will they? I mean if everyone did it to themselves they'd be out of business wouldn't they?"

Silence.

Then they changed the subject.

"Isabel my darling," Lance smiled, "did you see the guy with them two women? He was wearing his button shirt outside his trousers."

"I saw it. Told ya, only pricks do that," she replied.

"Yep," Brad intruded, "he was a right cocksucker."

"Brad!" yelled Mom, "wash your foul mouth out. I've told you not to swear like that."

"But you swear sometimes Mom, we've all heard you," he complained.

"Yes, sometimes I do but using that word and the motherf* word is not swearing, they are obscenities," Mom said assuredly, "Normal swearing is for the partly ignorant and illiterate, obscenities are for the totally ignorant and illiterate. Only backward people pretending to be forward talk like that. It's a substitute for intelligence and ability. Don't do it. It's like wearing a button shirt outside your trousers or showing your underpants and the cleavage in your arse. Total ignorance. Do you know that clever people never have to work hard to make an impression. They already have."

Suddenly they were surrounded by four or five little kids. Charging around, screaming and laughing using people and places for hiding and dodging. The family smiled indulgently at first until the laughter stopped and high pitched excited screaming took over.

"Hey," Russ said, grinning, "give us a break guys, go and play somewhere else. Where's your mummy?"

One gorgeous little one pointed shyly over to a group drinking and joking a few tables away.

Another one, a boy of course, stuck out his tongue and said, "Daddy sent us to play over here see, so there," and they all ran around screaming again.

The family didn't know whether to be shocked or amused. They sort of got stuck between the two.

Aussie Mum broke the silence, "needs a bloody good hiding that one does," she said firmly, "needs to learn how to behave. Disrespect starts early and kids, especially boys don't listen to reason. In one ear and out the other. The more you tell 'em the more bored they get with the message and still take no notice. Those who think you can reason with kids either never 'ad 'em or live over the rainbow. They need to take a walk down the yellow brick road. No wonder there's more crime, more disrespect and more violence. A parents job is to turn little animals into human beings. By the looks of that lot over there the success rate is low."

"The parents are just gabbing, yak yakking and drinking the whole time, not paying attention," said Jeanette, "anyway why are the kids up so late? They do need a good hiding."

"Who," asked Cooper, "the parents or the kids."

"Both," said Mum, "all of them are a bloody disgrace. Probably horrified at corporal punishment. You know the type. All hoity toity.

No one better touch my child at the same time as their kids are into total destruction."

"Yeah," agreed Mom, "any sensible person knows the difference between brutality and correction. For crissakes even lions do but we don't. A mother lion can kill with one sweep of her paw and claws or crush with huge jaws yet picks up cubs in her mouth, shakes them if unruly or gives them a swift cuff round the ears if out of hand. The cubs feel it, get the message, but are not permanently damaged. We can't seem to grasp the subtleties any more. It's what comes from letting the wrong people tell us what to do and how to behave."

"Well they just screamed and ran off," said Lance, "one banged her head on a table and another crashed into a chair. Most of 'em crying their eyes out. Got the attention of the parents though, didn't it?"

"What made them run off like that," asked Jeanette.

Brad looked embarrassed, "all I did was smile at them and offered the horrible kid a beer, being nice like. They all screamed and ran off."

"Well I think that children are lovely. It's horrible parents who make horrible kids," said Jeanette.

"Dunno about that," chuckled Brad, "we didn't turn out so bad did we?"

That was it, he was in trouble again.

"The problem with some people is that they can be a little too provocative," proclaimed Isabel, "get's you angry."

"Sometimes much too provocative and much too angry," said Mom.

"Know what you mean," said Brad, "when violence seems good."

"No it doesn't," Jeanette argued, "violence is never good. I don't mean a twist of the ear or a slap on the wrist to correct. I mean violent violence."

"Yeah, a lot need Anger Management," Pop chimed in, "learn a bit of control."

"How the hell do you do that?" asked Cooper, "I mean is there a therapist and what do they say? Do they pompously pronounce, 'I say old chap, not quite the way to behave is it?'"

"Could do aversion therapy couldn't they," Brad came in licking his lips, "Like electric shocks on mice. Maybe it needs cattle prods on humans eh?"

"You'd think that with all our great advances and discoveries they'd invent remedies like that though, wouldn't you?" said Russ, "you know, implants to deter bad behaviour. They've got implants to keep things going, so why not to stop things happening?"

"Oh I like that," laughed Isabel, "make going shopping or watching sports a whole lot more entertaining. Just imagine a guy thinking of rape and he gets a mental kick in the goolies or is made to vomit instead of hurting someone."

She was warming up, "yep how about getting a kick up the arse if contemplating stealing or being forced to immediately pray if thinking lewd thoughts. The shopping mall would become a full time entertainment centre."

"How about getting a great big protruding horn on if you fancy the woman next to you," said Brad eagerly.

"Oh for god's sake that happens to you anyway," said Lance, "you don't need implants."

"Some men need more than implants," said Mom, "you know the violent ones. The ones who beat up and torture their wives and kids."

"Beats me why they stay though," said Brad.

"Fear mate, fear," said Cooper, "fear of the guy, fear of being alone, fear of the unknown, fear of being unloved. All fear."

"Double standards though," Brad just had to come in, "women do beat up and bully men ya know, men also get raped."

"All right, maybe, but not nearly as often though, do they," cried Jeanette.

"Who knows, not reported is it?" replied Brad, "the men suffer a double whammy. They're not only terrified of the bullying but they're also ashamed. And as for rape. Well! A lot of sympathy they get. A man gang raped. Paradise man, sheer paradise. A fantasy come alive."

They were getting tired now so they all nodded in agreement.

They had been drinking solidly into the early hours of the morning and decided against anyone driving back to the Gold Coast.

The pub had a few spare rooms so they took them and slept in late the next day. They missed breakfast, had a late lunch and quietly journeyed back home. Hangovers were felt all round.

Nobody felt the need to put the world to rights.

Jeanette tried to revive their flagging spirits.

"Okay folks," she said spritely, "anyone got any ideas on the meaning of life. What's it all about then?"

She looked around expectantly.

No one responded or showed any interest until Brad said, "that's easy ain't it. You're either food or fertiliser. There's nothing else to it. Any species that don't supply it or can't get it just dies out. Survival of the species buddy, survival of the species."

No one challenged him. This time they were all too grateful to him. His answer was good enough particularly in the state they were in.

Brad was the hero for a change.

Sexy Sister Susie

Sister Susie suddenly appeared before them breathless. This was unusual. Susie was normally cool, calm and collected. Not this time. She was excited.

Although the family looked at her expectantly nothing came out.

They looked again.

Still nothing.

"Okay lady muck," smiled Russ, "what's going on. Don't make out all coy and girlie. We know you're just bursting to tell us. What's with the secrecy all of a sudden?"

"Well alright then, its just not me really, and you'd better not laugh. Promise?" she said, hesitantly.

"How can we promise anything when we don't know what the hell it is?" Cooper said a little scathingly, "bloody stupid when people say that, ain't it?

If it's that Daffy Duck then don't say it. Right? I mean what do you expect? Of course we're going to bloody well laugh aren't we? It's the same as saying that we'd never believe it, or you'll never guess, so you can't say, and then you say it anyway. 'Cos you were always going to. Crazy girl, crazy!"

"Well I won't tell you then," she said petulantly.

"Great, so we can move on then can we," said Russ.

"Oh all right, I'll tell you," Susie said quickly.

"Why the hell do we have to go through this nonsense so often, it's kids stuff, right?" said Cooper, "get on with it then. Jesus women do go on, don't they? Gabbing on and on about nothing much at all. Clack, clack, clack, gossip, gossip, gossip. When they run out of their own nonsense they switch on TV to see what someone else is gossiping about."

"Yeah, know what you mean bro," said Brad, trying to look intelligent and involved, "had a girlfriend once, a real babe, but she just wouldn't and couldn't shut up. Went on and on and on. The only time she was quiet was when she was sucking my dick and even then she was mumbling."

"Huh! Knowing you," chuckled Jeanette, "she was either saying don't shove so hard you're choking me or she was complaining don't you ever wash this thing?"

"When you've finished with all your dirty talk I'd like to hear what my daughter has to say, if you don't mind," Mum said primly.

Everyone shut up with sheepish expressions on their faces and looked once again expectantly at Susie.

She hesitated until Cooper blurted out, "oh for fucks sake she's been struck dumb again. Get on with it."

She said slowly, "I know guys fancy me because I'm never short of offers, but I don't fancy myself as being a beauty. No, no, it's alright," she said in order to stifle the protests from her brothers and especially from Brad, "I've always been comfortable with what I am."

"Right," said Cooper abruptly, "got that, where you going with it next?"

"Well a group came up to me along the beach area, cameras an' all, and asked if I could spare them a few moments, so I did," she said smugly, "they were part of a tele production team. Their van was just over the road. They wanted local, not tourist input."

"Sooo?" said Russ, encouragingly with a question in his voice.

"So, they want to do a few seconds clip of me dancing, sort of local stuff, show what's going on here like. Do you reckon I should?" she asked somewhat plaintively.

"Dancing! You dancing on tele?" Cooper shrieked, laughing his head off, "what sort of dancing? The Wallaby Waltz or the Kangaroo Can Can?"

"See, I said you'd laugh, didn't I? Said it wasn't quite me, didn't I?" she said accusingly.

"And we said we would laugh," said Russ grinning, "so seriously, what's the dance because you have to admit you're hardly MGM Hollywood material are you?"

"Hula, Hula, South Sea Island dancing, that's what," Susie said, at last defiant.

"What!" exclaimed Cooper, "that's not very local is it? I've seen the Abo's and us doing some fancy movements but we leave things like Hula Hula to the Maoris don't we? You know the lot who stamp their feet and poke their tongues out at you thinking it scares you off."

"Fucking rude if you ask me," said Brad, "the only thing scary about that is that they think it scary."

"Well they were separated from the rest of the world for years, weren't they," Russ chuckled, "lost a bit of touch I reckon. Thought warfare was still a bit of a kid's game. Then along came the White Man with his guns and boom boom, out go the lights."

"Yeah they lost," Cooper said laconically.

"And you reckon women prattle on," said Isabel, "just listen to yourselves. Talk about the pot calling the kettle black."

"Watch it, you're bound to offend somebody just queueing up to be offended. They'll say that's rascist," said Pop, attempting humour, unusually for him.

"Okay then. I'll say people in glass houses shouldn't throw stones. Is that better?" asked Isabel.

"Nope," replied Jeanette, "the politically correct will say that it incurs the hint of violence."

"Oh go and fuck them all," said Isabel in exasperation, "the lunatics really have taken over the asylum. Do you have to dress up Susie, you know, like in costume?"

"Yes, of course. It's a bit revealing but I thought I looked good," Susie said boldly but at the same time trying to seem modest, "I accepted by the way. It's all done and dusted. I get five thousand dollars from the tourist board and keep the costume."

"Bloody hell, I'd do it for that," said Isabel, as excited as Susie.

"Hold on girl," said Lance, "for someone your size they'd have to pay double."

"Twice the reason then," said Isabel, "when can we see you dressed in costume Susie? When do we get a demo?"

"Right away, I'll go and change now," she said, and promptly disappeared.

"Blimey, that was a quick decision," Russ said, "god only knows what she'll look like."

When she came out they were dumbstruck. She did look good, she did look sexy. Brad was horny for weeks just remembering it and she danced well.

Nobody laughed.

"What do you think," she asked a little shyly and hesitantly"

"What do you think?" she said a little shyly and hesitantly. She was usually a tough self-assured cookie so this humility and femininity took them all by surprise. She was not one to go all girlie and didn't think much of women who presented themselves with sexuality upfront. She believed in personality and if it came over sexy as well then that was a bonus.

Brad broke the silence, "if I didn't know it was you I'd fancy you and come out with my favourite chat up line."

"What's that then?" she asked.

"I defy scientific description," he said proudly, "how's that?"

"Thank god you know me then," she said with relief, "however there's someone I met there who I didn't know before and you don't know now. I want you to meet."

"Great, if she looks like you, I can't wait," Brad cried.

"Hey, she's not a she, she's a he," laughed Susie, "sorry to disappoint you."

"Ah well," said Russ, "if he's impressed you then I'm sure we'll be impressed too. You know the drill. Any friend of yours is a friend of ours."

"I've always found that first impressions count," Brad said wisely, "then the rot sets in. The longer you know someone the less you like them. Divorce is a great invention. You get in, you get on, you get off and then you get out."

"There speaks the great philosopher," laughed Lance, "my brother Plato. He said that what we call learning is only a process of recollection."

"Who, what?" asked Russ, "your brother said that?"

"No, you idiot," laughed Lance, "Plato. My brother is more in line with the Buddha who said the mind is everything, what you think you become. I reckon that says everything about Brad."

"Hello, I'm still here you know," Susie said impatiently, "does anyone want to meet my friend?"

"Yeah, go girl, get him in. Where is he?" cried Isabel.

"I'll give him a call, we can meet up later," she replied, "if that's okay with everyone."

All agreed.

"Excuse me," Russ said, "but can I suggest that you change first. You would make some of the guys eyes pop out in the bars we go to. They'd be queueing up to buy you a drink, take your order and stroke your butt if you looked like that. They would not take kindly to you or your friend knocking them flat on their backs in reply."

"Huh," Susie sneered mockingly, "if you're talking about the guys you hang around with then they wouldn't know the difference between a knockout or a hangover. Both ways they end up flat on their backs. Let's go."

The Friend

The family were very early for the meet. It was so unusual for Susie to be upfront about a boy. They didn't want to miss a second.

Susie very rarely brought anyone home. Not since college. She was too conscious of her brothers sizing them up. If her friends were girls they acted the fool in front of them and if they were boys they came on all macho.

As Susie didn't really go for brawn or beauty her choices of men or women rarely suited her brothers.

When she confronted them after a number of disastrous introductions they assured her that they were only joking and they really liked the guys and girls. Then came that all too revealing word 'but'. She believed that little word and its alternatives always revealed the true feelings. She thought it probably the most important word ever uttered. I'm not rascist but ----- I'm not prejudiced but --- I get on very well with him but --- although he's right I think that ---- I'd go willingly however ----!

She couldn't wait to introduce this young man. He was a whacky, off the wall events organiser. She just knew he was not going to go down at all well.

She arrived alone.

The family couldn't hide their disappointment.

"Where is he sis?" asked Cooper looking about furtively thinking he was funny, "stood you up has he? Seen us and gone into hiding?"

"You wish," she said, "he's just had to wind up a rehearsal for a ceremony. He'll be here shortly."

Almost before she finished speaking a wild looking, athletic guy, bounded into the hotel lounge, leaped a chair and said, "hello."

He swept Susie into his arms rakishly, knowing exactly what he was doing, smiled and kissed her passionately.

Her brothers waited for the explosion to come from either Mum or Susie.

They looked amazed. Mum was smiling indulgently and Susie was beaming at the same time as wriggling closer in.

"Idiot," laughed Susie, "trust you. Let me introduce you properly."

And she did.

"Sorry for being a bit late," he said, "I had to confirm some arrangements for a Bar Mitzvah. For a kid ya know. A Jewish kid."

"Yeah we know," said Lance, "are you Jewish then?"

"Sort of," he said, "you know what it's like. There are no religious kids in the world. What religion they take is decided by their parents before they've any opinions on the matter. Trapped for life."

"Are you trapped then?" asked Pop.

"Sort of. I'm non practising," he replied.

Mum chuckled, "oh my goodness what a world we live in. My son is married to a non practising catholic and my daughter is going out with a non practising jew. I bet you don't practice non practising sex."

"No one worries these days Mum," said Russ, "I mean look, America has a coloured President. Things have changed."

"Not that much," interrupted Isabel, "the day the good old US of A elects a Jewish President then things will really have changed. There are those who would support a foreign, murdering dictator but couldn't stomach a Jewish President and as for a Muslim, well, forget it."

"Unfortunately true," said Lance, "We have friends who say they are not anti semitic, just anti-zionist."

"It's like someone saying that they're not anti-American, just anti-America," said the young man whose name was David.

"I can understand that," said Brad with a serious expression, "I think my fellow Americans are great but America pisses me off sometimes."

David gave Brad a strange look. If he was going to hang around then he would have to get used to him.

The family ignored him.

Unfortunately Brad was warming up. He was experiencing a warm glow of friendship.

"All these so called important people struggle over finding a solution in the Middle East. It's easy. Just bloody well recognise Israel and let everyone settle down. Then the Arabs can be like the old time Europeans before they formed the EU. Get down to the real business of killing each other off without the Jewish excuse and diversion until they come to a similar conclusion to the westerners. Form their own union so they can blame each other without fighting. Mind you they'd probably end up like the Europeans and fuck it all up."

He looked around totally satisfied with himself.

There was a complete silence which he really felt the urge to fill. So he went on, "And as for that lot called the United Nations. Should be called the Disunited Nations. It's nothing but a Talkfest. Lies, propaganda, spin, contradictions and bullshit."

"Better jaw jaw than war war," said Lance.

"Yeah, but it's not jaw jaw anymore is it?" he said. "It's bore bore! Man alive, with education, meducation and relief they really try but Peacekeepin', my gawd, call it Peacekeeping. A joke man. The peacekeeping forces are usually made up from unaligned neutral countries which means they usually don't fight. So they don't. Leave too many in the lurch to die. What about committees? Excuses for publicly doing nuttin'. Nuttin at all, except posing for photos with other gabby do nothings. Some agree, some disagree and most don't care. It's like all information and think tanks - if crap goes in then crap comes out. We all deserve better and don't anyone say that we get what we deserve or I'll kick arse."

Nobody did.

"Blimey!" exclaimed Isabel, "I reckon talking about religion is safer than Brad mouthing off on world affairs."

"Are you religious then," asked David.

"Nah," said Isabel, "I'm like most people. Believe when it suits me. Shrug it off when it doesn't. Frankly all I want from God is the assurance that all those poor dead children who never had a chance of life are growing up happy in heaven."

"Enough," cried Mom, "what sort of a welcome is this for Susie's friend? Come on, let's have some laughter. Where are the jokes?"

"I've got some," said Brad eagerly, then looked around, "wait a moment, where you all going?"

"We're not just going," said Jeanette, "we're running away like crazy."

The family thought that was funny. Suddenly they were laughing.

David later kept them amused with disasters that happened during events.

The favourite was the one where he had to deal with a great rock star bombed out of his mind on drink and drugs before he was due to go on stage. He had no idea where he was or what he was doing until his Roadies put his guitar in his hands. He became docile, let them lead him on stage where he suddenly exploded into action. He performed brilliantly for three hours straight with encores, seemingly in command. As soon as he came off stage he collapsed surrounded by baffled medics until a groupie shoved through and sloshed some vodka down his throat. He quickly came round and staggered off with a few groupies, holding a bottle, asking over his shoulder as he went, "where the fuck am I?" Because of so many similar incidents the rock star was given a minder to keep him off the drink and drugs. The problem was that the minder was an alcoholic!!

During a lull in the hilarity it occurred to Cooper to ask what it was that David actually did, and how did he get into it. He was intrigued. Susie normally went cerebral. What was it with this one when so many had been sent packing. They usually disappeared quicker than a fart in a field, he thought.

"What do you do then mate?" he asked, a bit more sharply than he had intended.

David blinked, looked directly at him, and replied, "you know what I do. We've been talking about it for the past half hour."

A wild, athletic young man charged into the lounge, leaping a chair as he came.

"Yeah, I know, sorry like. What I meant was, how did you get into it? You know, one day Bar Whatsits and the next rock concerts," he mumbled, all embarrassed, "I mean we don't see many job adverts in that line, do we?"

"Contacts man, contacts," David said, "I gotta degree in Constructional Engineering, helped out some pals in college who were forming a rock band and while applying for jobs I started as a roadie for them stuffing equipment into an old van and setting it up. As they grew so did I and the work. Soon I was their event planner and it got bigger and more complicated as did the gigs and sets. In between I was recommended for other festivals, earning good money and no longer looking for work. The weddings, bar mitzvahs and birthdays I do as a favour. You know what parents are like. 'Talk to my boy, he'll do it. He's the best. He's not as boring as a doctor, dentist or lawyer. He's exciting and successful. So successful, makes money.' Makes me cringe sometimes but what the hell!"

"I knew it," cried Russ, "brains and brawn. Our Susie's not daft."

"Huh, you didn't know it. Ya were just as confused as I was," Cooper grinned, "you're like everyone. Know it all in hindsight."

"Yeah," smiled Brad, eager to get his bit in again, "you know what the definition of hindsight is don't ya? It means looking and talking out of your arse. You get it? Hind means backside and sight means well sight? Easy 'ennit? Well it is when you're in the know. I reckon hindsight is just passing through. Like wind after eating baked beans."

David glanced over at him and declared, "this guy is good. Wish I could work things out like he does. Perhaps you could call him an original."

"Perhaps you could call him a lot of things and we do. He's actually accepted that he defies scientific definition. Likes and uses that as a chat up line," Lance said sardonically.

"Does it work?" asked David.

"Nope, fails every time," Isabel said, "but he still won't give up."

"Hey! Hold on a moment. The girls just lacked perception, that's all," Brad cried, "any gal with enough edification would see it immediately. They don't see into me is all."

"You're right, they don't see into you bro," Lance laughed, "they see through you, that's the point."

Brad seemed about to explode but subsided instead.

He felt misunderstood and unappreciated. It was not a good feeling.

Isabel sensed it and sympathised. But she knew that it would not be long before Brad opened his mouth again and put his foot in it. More like a mile than a foot.

They all had a clear idea about David but how much did David know about them? Brad, maybe, was not the best example of cool.

"I know a whole lot about you," David said, as if he had heard the unspoken question, "Susie told me buckets."

"Did she?" Russ said ominously, "didn't think she had that much time."

"Yep, sure did," David replied, apparently oblivious to the tone of Russ's voice, "a very hot, fast worker, you're sister. Most girls are now you know. Wow!" He winked at Jeanette.

The two Mum's did not like the sound of that at all. They glanced at each other then glared at David. He got the message. Too many parents and too many macho brothers in the present company.

"I meant fast talker of course," he said hastily, "you know, girls aren't slow in coming forward. Expect to be able to talk about themselves instead of just obediently listening to the man showing off." He faded out lamely.

"I agree with you man, a guy can't get a word in," it was Brad who came to the rescue, "before you even take a sip of your beer you even know what Neanderthal cave her ancestors came from."

David looked at him gratefully even though he seemed an unreliable ally. He hesitated.

He was right to pause.

Encouraged, Brad continued, "yeah, the old days were better. Kill mammoth with mates, pig out, feel horny, pick up club, leave cave, find female, bash her with club, drag her into cave and fuck madly without interruption. Paradise man, simply paradise. Ah pity those good old days are no more." He sighed.

Isabel also sighed, "thank god for no more dimwit troglodytes."

"Yeah," said Brad, "I agree. Electricity is so much better."

He genuinely missed out on the incredulous looks flashing around the families. He was used to it. He had unfortunately become immune.

He would never intentionally be difficult or hurtful, he did it all accidentally.

The Aussies started to talk about football, the World Cup, Asian Cup and other contests. Australia did well considering population and distances.

They had players in most of the major European leagues and got pretty fair results. They did, unlike many Asian countries, have a tradition of male and female athletes, continually as World class stars. The Yanks joined in. They, like the British, had pride in their achievements. They had to continually have someone up there somewhere in most events. They worked hard at it.

The conversation turned to the advances in technology.

Virtually every sport had embraced it and were continually upgrading. Except football.

"Fucking corrupt old dinosaurs in charge, that's why," smirked Cooper, "all full of stupid ideas letting the good ones get away."

"Yeah, that leader, what's his name? Sleep Better, that's it, Sleep Better. He don't know his arse from his elbow, poor ol' fucker," chuckled Russ, "said technology would take the passion out of the game, silly old bugger. He's so old he's forgotten what it is."

"He mistakes passion for anger, frustration and irritation at continual bad decisions and inconsistencies that could be overcome by technology," Isabel joined in excitedly, "Rugby, cricket, tennis, athletics, and tons of others use it without any loss at all. In fact they are better for it. Football would be too."

"But don't you think that there'd be too many stoppages?" Pop asked quietly.

"Oh for crissakes, Dad," Cooper laughed, "get real. There are stoppages all the time. Never heard off kick offs, goals, off sides, injuries, free kicks, corners, throw ins, penalties, fouls, yellow cards, red cards, disputes and half time? Technology makes for better decisions that's all. Crazy that the tele viewers at home can see what really happened in replay seconds later but the officials can't. The sport is run by out of date, out of touch short sighted fogies, only interested in their own power and survival. Football welfare comes well down on the list."

"They reckon that they can't find reliable enough technology," Pop tried again.

"Of course THEY say that. THEY would, wouldn't THEY! Of course nothing's perfect but how come the other sports found it all okay. No co-incidence that there's much less violence in the other sports, even the violent ones."

"It is still the most beautiful game in the world though isn't it," Pop said ruefully.

"Of course Dad," Russ assured him, encouragingly, "but it would be even more fair and beautiful if it were run better. Do we all agree?"

"We all agree, so do most fans the world over. Probably everyone except the morons in charge," replied Isabel, "to me it seems to be a sport that grows in popularity in spite of, rather than because of, those who profess to love it and control it."

"That's because it's a poor man's game where you can become rich. Too many sports were for those who had money in the first place. You know, the old fashioned rubbish - gentlemen and players. So many looked down on those who worked for a living. Football was founded by those who had to work for a living, no choice mate," said Brad, "helped by the tele later of course."

Everyone was astounded. Brad of all people, who genuinely, but mistakenly, thought football was called soccer, had finally said something they could almost all agree on.

"Bloody hell," thought Isabel, along with the others, "miracles do happen."

They decided to go for a walk along the waterfront. It was noisy, hot and busy but there was a refreshing breeze blowing in from the sea.

Isabel and Lance had missed the sound of the sea. They savoured it, felt it and smelled it, taking in huge breaths deep down.

They were starting to miss home.

Susie suddenly stopped, "bloody hell, a bird dropped his load and just missed me. Landed splat on my bag. Do they do it on purpose out of revenge and disrespect, aren't any of them house trained?" She frantically scrubbed at her bag with tissues.

"Do you know what I think?" said Isabel, "I reckon birds are nearly as bad as governments and tycoons. They spread shit on everyone everywhere. Don't care where it lands as long as it's not on them."

"Go girl, go," laughed Lance, "we haven't heard from Wunderwear Woman for ages. Let it rip."

"Who the hell is this Wunderwear person," asked David, clearly bewildered.

"Wunderwear is really my wife Isabel pal," explained Lance, "or perhaps it's the other way round. Whenever she gets stirred up about something, and I mean really stirred up, then Isabel changes into Wunderwear Woman, the protector of the downtrodden millions."

"Wow," exclaimed David, "I spout a bit here and there about injustice but I can't fly or anything."

"Neither can Wunderwear Woman," chuckled Lance, "that's what makes her unique."

"You should hear her sometimes. You might be able to hold Isabel back but you'd stand no chance with Wunderwear once she gets going," said Mom, "I just love that feisty gal. Got spirit."

"She likes the free market as long as it's not closed to most. She understands the need for capital as long as too much is not accumulated in one place.

She loves enterprise as long as it's not crushed by oppression of any sort and realises that a democratic government has a major and not minor role to play in people's lives. She understands that all people are initially created in an equal way but not with equal attributes. She believes that not all luck is created by preparation and that not all opportunity is created by luck. Far too simplistic and unreal," Lance reeled off and then paused for breath, "go on darling, tell 'em of your latest pet hate."

"Privatisation," Wunderwear giggled, "it's an ideology, not an economic reality. Private enterprise makes money and survives from profit, not taxation. It exists for the prime benefit of the owners. Yes it is entrepreneurial but any benefit that comes the way of customers is secondary. Important yes, but secondary. It used to follow the market but now the market follows it. Public ownership survives from taxation, can make money, but its prime objective is the common good."

Therefore schools should educate the young workers of the future. The better educated the better chance of them being useful and productive members of society later on. That should be the objective and ideal. Not making a fast buck for a few now and making financial survival the main aim.

The same with doctors, clinics and hospitals. They should exist to make all people fit and well to go back into the workforce. Not attempt to compete for the highest earners and payers.

Just imagine. Privatised schools competing for pupils by making people ignorant longer so as to keep them in expensive education longer! Doesn't happen. Well I reckon Eton, Harrow, Harvard and Yale have been doing it for years.

Fancy privatised hospitals having a festival of accidents day so as to get more paying customers in because business has slacked off!

Impossible, oh yeah!? Not in this screwed up world.

What you say? Oh yeah, poorer people would take advantage of free medicine for perhaps trivial things. Yeah well maybe, but for sure poorer people can't take advantage of free medicine for serious things 'cos they bloody well can't afford it. So keep everyone out except the rich whether they're ill or not. Oh they say, I'm traumatised because of the shape of my nose. I've got money so I must, just must, get it fixed. I can't live with it as it is. But fucking tough luck on a poor person who's got cancer!!??

Can you see privatised fire brigades having a 'Light a Fire Day.' Read Mr Bradbury's, is that his name, book about Fahrenheit something or other? Pure genius. Or ambulance brigades canvassing for a 'Bad Crash Day' because they're not busy making enough money.

Just picture privatised railways using up valuable countryside racing side by side competing on more or less the same routes. Won't happen? Perhaps not but what about airlines then?!!

Let's have differently owned expensive privatised buses clamouring for customers in busy cities with different systems clogging up the traffic and persecute cars instead. Doesn't happen. Try London.

Travel on privatised trains which do not compete for routes because a nutcase government decided that one company could own the trains, another the stations and another the track and systems. Couldn't happen? Shouldn't happen? Then don't elect ignoramus arch conservatives such as Maggie Thatcher.

Private prisons. Yeah, let's convict more. Let's support zero tolerance. Create more prisons. Create criminals more resentful so they come back again. Nothing like a satisfied customer! Maybe you could shoot more of them as they surrender. Saves money all round. Only in the good ol' US of A you think? Well, maybe mainly there today but could be all over tomorrow. One supposedly more civilised country shot and killed an innocent student while he was lying helpless on the floor of a train. Thought he was a terrorist. Strikes me there was not much thinking done. The people who did it should never be allowed to go within ten miles of a weapon again, let alone take any responsibility.

Private post, there's one for you. Write a longer letter day. Only one collection and delivery a month because you live in a unprofitable area or go and collect your own from ten miles away even if you're old and disabled. Why not? Dr. Beeching did it with railways in the UK.

Private police forces. Didn't we use to call them bodyguards or vigilantes once?"

Hey look, we need to take power away from those who do no good, make crap decisions benefitting the few and make sure we elect people who want to make it work. What sort of politician talks of less government, less help, less aid and less everything when there's more poverty and millions more unemployed. Have you noticed how those who call for less government are the most keen to get in it? Who in their right mind would elect such people thinking such things were a solution. A solution to what? Why not make enterprise and bureaucracy work well, balanced, and side by side. Privatisation is all too often an obsession not necessarily a benefit. Elect good people, caring people.

For fucks sake why does nobody want to understand that in a world of over six billion population with global communication and expectation open to everyone such inequality, despair and unrestricted laissez-faire is lessez quality for all in the end. It's a bloody recipe for disaster.

For goodness sake elect governments from the people, by the people and for the people. Didn't a great man say that once some time ago? Of course he did. So why not bloody well go ahead and do it?"

"Yep, so don't vote Republican then," said Mom. She just couldn't resist it as Wunderwear paused for breath.

Everyone laughed and waited for more.

There was none.

Wunderwear Woman was done for now.

"Atta girl," cried Lance.

"Amen," sighed the Aussies.

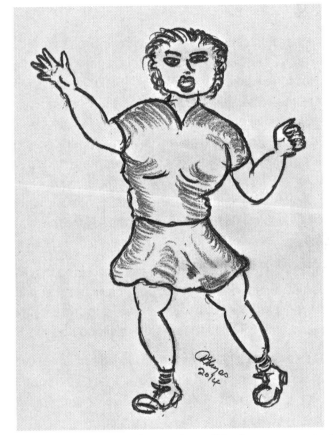

Have you noticed how those who call for less government
are the most keen to get in it?

Winding up, Winding down!

"Hey," shouted David, "there's a couple of my mates over there. I'll just shoot over there for a minute, okay?"

Before anyone could answer he was there and back.

"All right if we meet up tomorrow for lunch?" he asked.

"David, you don't have to ask us for permission to meet your pals, you're a free agent man," said Russ.

"Not quite," Susie interjected with a frown.

"No, no, no," David replied with a smile, "I mean all of us. I'd love you to meet them, they're great. You know, a bit of my friends being your friends, sort of thing?"

The family were uncertain. Seemed a bit of too much too early.

"Please guys," David pleaded, "you'll like 'em. That's if it's okay of course. I've told 'em you're great folks."

"Well I suppose," said Mum reluctantly, "if it's okay with everyone that is."

There were reluctant nods all round.

"Great, thanks a lot," he said before shooting off and returning quickly again, "all fixed. One o'clock here at that fish restaurant over the road. You'll love it. See ya. Lovely to meet you." He kissed Susie and ran off.

Russ and Cooper were puzzled. Susie was usually very dominant and quite normally unco-operative in a relationship. Here she was just happy to go along with it.

Susie caught the glances between the two.

"Don't worry. He's a great guy but all over the place. He's like the big fish we let run a bit before reeling it in," she said, "if I reckon he's worth it later I'll soon bring him into line."

"Phew," chuckled Cooper, "we were worried there for a while."

"Don't be," Susie said firmly, "we can only do what we gotta do, and maybe I'm gonna do him. We'll see what happens. At the moment I don't want to get involved too much. I find that one of the most superficial things anyone can say is 'get real' because they always seem to be the most unreal of the lot.

Anyway real reality is unbearable. Who wants to take a close, revealing look at themselves. Disaster, no way, too painfull, hardest thing of all. You always want to point the finger the other way, never at yourself. I reckon that's what suicides are really all about. They take a too serious look at reality especially their own. Can't face it. I mean Brad is a perfect example of what happens when you get close and ask what someone has on their mind. Mostly you don't wanna know."

If Brad heard he gave no indication.

He seemed to be somewhere else.

The family held their breath.

Something was coming and they didn't have long to wait.

"I had a thought," he said-----

"Wow," interrupted the family altogether, "hold onto it Brad. Don't let it escape. If it's any good we'll get you a star on that pavement in Hollywood."

"Yeah let the dogs pee on it all the time," laughed Cooper, "fancy wanting half the world to walk all over you everyday. You'd have to be in movies to think it good."

"Dunno though," grinned Russ, "get to look up a lot of women's legs wouldn't you?"

" As I was saying," Brad said patiently, "it's clear to me that Susie's one of them there girls who don't just want to be equal but want to rule."

We don't need to do equal things all the time to be equal.
Let the most suitable qualified people be free strut their
stuff whatever their race, sex, religion, age or colour.

Before Susie could jump on him Russ interjected, "perhaps they feel the need to redress the balance."

"What balance?" Brad cried mockingly, "if they had any sense they'd turn the clock backwards wouldn't they? Those old time gals had it made and the further back you go the mader they had it."

"Whaat!?" screamed Wunderwear, "how do you get from here to there being better for goodness sake?"

"Well smart old time woman said to dumb old time hunk,' you heap big strong man, you go out and be brave and face all the dangers. Me poor, weak little woman, me stay safe in cave and light fire. Sister says to woman, 'did dumbo go for it?!' 'Yeah,' says woman, 'now tell me all about that slut in the cave next door.' And the men fell for it for years.

Dumb hunk gets killed. Smart woman cuddles up to new man. If they carry on being equal they will soon die the same as us and where would all the tours and cruises be without all the horny widows?"

Silence at first.

Then.

"What about all the deaths at childbirth. Women died young then didn't they?" asked Mom, surprisingly calmly.

"Of course," said Brad expansively, "that's 'cos they had all those 'orrible harridans full of superstitious crap as midwives didn't they? Still do when men can't attend to them. They only started to live when men got involved."

"So what's the thought then bro?" asked Lance, "there must be one in there somewhere."

"Yeah, 'course there is, told you didn't I?" Brad said, sounding exasperated, "humans need men and women to make new humans, right? Humans need men and women together to survive, right. So we're all equal really anyway aren't we? We don't need to do equal things all the time to prove it. Let the most suitable people free to do their stuff whatever the sex, race, religion or colour.

"Eureka!" cried Wunderwear, "he's got there at last. He's got it, by jove I think he's got it! Took longer than Eliza Doolittle, but he's got it."

"Yeah, hallelujah," Jeanette laughed happily, "my brother's gone from proper prick to philosopher, from poet to politician. Five p's in a row. Previously he only got than many p's from a few gallons of beer."

Happy days.

They refocussed.

They were all intent on dinner, a relaxing drink and bed.

Tomorrow wasn't just another day. It was the second to last day of the visit.

Rainbow Men

Nobody said too much at breakfast. They were not really looking forward to the lunch date but they didn't want to upset Susie.

They took their time getting ready. Lethargy was the order of the day.

They decided to walk to the restaurant to work up an appetite and maybe to stimulate a little enthusiasm.

It worked. Well sort of. The mood certainly improved.

By the time they arrived they were almost upbeat.

"Right Susie girl," said Russ, stretching his arms and taking a deep breath, "new day, new friends, let's bring it on."

"Do you know something?" said Cooper, "just occurred to me, a bit late I know, but well better late than never, so they say."

"What a load of rubbish," laughed Russ, "who cares what they bloody well say. I want to know what you say. So for goodness sake spit it out. Get on with it."

"Well, we've bin with a load of yanks now for quite a while, ain't we?" said Cooper, "and do you know what? I haven't heard one of 'em say, oh my gawd, awesome, shucks, gee whizz or God save America."

"Also no one has kept on using the word 'like' three times in every sentence," said Russ, "like in like."

"Oh only emerging stars keep on saying like." laughed Mom, "they think it makes them sound young and fresh."

"Makes 'em sound illiterate to me," said Isabel smugly, "anyway the reason the Yanks here aren't using all those lame expressions is because of my British influence."

"Ha, bloody ha!" laughed Brad, managing to sound only a little false, "you wish."

"Don't tempt me," Isabel said lightly, "I might get what I wish for. Even though I believe that you have to be careful what you wish for. There's no telling when or where you might appear again. At least we know where you are now."

"Yeah, we can sort of keep an eye on him," said Mom, "he's one of those you need to keep close. You worry if he leaves the nest."

"Huh he needs to do that every time he gets broody," said Lance, "as long as his chickens don't come home to roost."

"Hey, cut it out," cried Brad, "there's more corn there than in the mid-west.

If you're going to have a go at me then for fucks sake try a bit of originality."

Isabel groaned, "corn he says, when we've been talkin' about chickens and roosting. That really is corny."

"Cut it out," Mom chuckled, "this is going downhill. Let's go in."

So they did.

Meet the Band - The Rainbow Men.

Modern Bollywood Seventies Man.   Punk   Mr. D'Arcy.

and Buddha who is missing contemplating his navel.

David was already there with three friends, tables reserved and pushed together. They made a crowd.

They were all introduced to each other at the same time as the staff were hovering and sorting so it took a while to get organised. Hands were shaken and missed, hugs were attempted and failed and air kisses kissed air. One or two of the female staff got welcomed warmly by Brad who took advantage of the chaos and pretended to mistake them for David's friends. One was so enthusiastic and forward she made Brad step backward wincing. Cooper who saw it was not surprised as she was definitely in Brad's so called preferred age group. He nodded encouragement at Brad.

"Reckon you're in there man," he managed to say in amongst the melee, "go and make her spill the soup."

"No way," Brad said hotly, "she crushed my balls and said too small little one, far too small."

"do you mean she got all that from just one feel," Cooper smiled, "what a woman. That's what I call some experience."

"That's what I call a bad one," grinned Brad.

Who was sitting where and next to who was hotly disputed although no one really cared that much. The elders being over solicitous and considerate the younger ones obliging by sitting and shoving in wherever.

Rudeness eventually solved the problem because those left standing and wondering had to fit into the spaces left over.

Wunderwear thought it typical of the world at large.

However she said nothing for a change and just sat down.

She looked around her taking in David's friends. They were not at all out of the same mould. Visually they didn't fit together at all. It wasn't just an obvious difference of race or colour. It was one of style.

They were all very individual.

One was Indian, a mixture of very Seventies and Bollywood forever. Another was punk thuggish and the other was elegant 19th century ponytail. Isabel was tempted to call him Mr. D'Arcy.

They were members of the rock band.

"Hum!" thought Isabel, she had pulled back Wunderwear so as to be reserved and polite at first, "rock stars don't become famous for their maturity and common sense so this could be interesting."

The length of the adjoined tables meant that conversations were local. One or two attempted to shout across, diagonally and up and down but gave up as soon everyone was trying it. Unsuccessfully of course.

The ordering and consumption of food took priority.

Isabel felt Wunderwear rising again as Susie attempted to advise her on what fish and seafood were preferable.

"Okay, thanks," she said, tartly, "but I'm in the business you know? It's our living."

"Yeah I know," Susie replied a bit patronisingly, "but knowing how best to catch'em doesn't mean you know how best to cook 'em does it?"

Isabel took a deep breath, "and knowing how to talk doesn't mean you know when it's best to shut up does it?"

"All right then," said Susie, in a bit off a huff, "only trying to help," and she turned away.

"Whoops," thought Isabel, "easy girl, it's the last day here and you are bristling over nothing much."

"Hey, just kidding," Isabel said, lightly punching Susie on the shoulder.

Isabel's light punches were never light. This one rocked Susie sideways.

"Wow," cried Susie, laughing, "how do you punch when you're angry?"

"Don't be around then kiddo," Isabel smirked self consciously, "I'm a demon."

Their attention was drawn to the words flying around further down the table. One of the guys had attempted to re-assure the older folks that maybe they were not going to die. A few scientists had said that they were close to a break through to ensure that everyone lived forever.

This was a conversation that Wunderwear could not resist. First off talking about death to middle aged or elderly people was not at all re-assuring no matter how you presented it. Secondly it was speculation.

"I saw that bearded pony tailed geyser on television once," she said, "all smug and full of himself. Seemed to think that presenting rubbish in a reasonable way was convincing. Full of himself and his superiority he was."

"We all saw it," said Lance, "reckoned that with a few breakthroughs we could all live forever, or anyways indefinitely. Same thing in the end I suppose."

"But no guarantees though," thundered Wunderwear, who couldn't resist emerging, "as always on tele it's maybe possible here and there but never possible in the here and now. If there's no guarantee what's the point?"

"I got one," said Brad, eagerly, "the point is we'd all like to live forever, so I say go for it prof!"

"Duh! Tough on those who miss out though 'ennit?" said Lance, "they're really gonna be pissed of ain't they. Oh yeah, you think you're gonna live for ever and I'm not. Bang, bang, you're dead brother same as me. Recipe for disaster if you ask me."

"Claimed it was not irresponsible to spend trillions on his research rather than on curing sickness and poverty," said Jeanette, "of course he smarmily showed off that he was in good health and he obviously wasn't poor. Bet he paid himself well. What a berk."

"Yeah, totally self-centered," Mom said, entering into the fray, "of course all the while claiming he wasn't."

"Well they do don't they?" said Brad, not wanting to be left out.

"He smartly dodged the question of over population and extra use of resources," cried Wunderwear, "dumped it all elsewhere by saying that there could well be other solutions by then. Oh yeah Mr. Smartass, give us some then. Yep, don't let's be sensible and far sighted," she exclaimed, "let's just be stupid and create more problems."

"He reckoned it was natural and not contrary to evolution," said Jeanette, "but if everything lived forever there wouldn't be any evolution would there?

Nothing would be going back to replenish the earth. As Brad said, we're here to feed and fertilise, that's the meaning of existence. Anyway Evolution would have got there by now without our help if it was okay, wouldn't it?"

Wunderwear said emphatically, "typical of a combination of education and gift of the gab without intelligence."

The usual silence followed.

Then, "perhaps he's just one of those self-centered scientists who live only for science. They always struggle to justify it," said Seventies Bollywood man, "they live in their own weird cloistered intellectual world. You know, we'll create a supposed solution for something that will become a problem for someone else to solve. Aren't we clever? And then they'll congratulate each other endlessly at the same time backstabbing any opposition."

Wunderwear smiled. She liked that.

David and his friends seemed stunned by the whirlwind that had taken off around them in seconds.

For the family it was SNAFU. Situation Normal All Fucked Up!

Aussie Mum of course had a personal interest in her in-laws who she had come to know quite well and actually like. They seemed real people. She was however even more interested in David and his friends at the moment. Susie, her beloved only daughter, head screwed on the right way, commonsense girl was involved with this lot.

She was continually looking so sharply left and right taking everything in that Isabel thought she was at Wimbledon.

Mum saw an opening, "why are you called The Rainbow Men?" she asked inquisitively, "you don't look like sticks of seaside rock to me? Is it because you're sweet or something? Don't ask me to lick you to find out or my husband will punch your lights out."

"Nah, nah," laughed D'Arcy, "we call ourselves that 'cos we're typical of globalisation. We're global us lot. All colours, all born and bred Australian but ethnically varied and have different religions. A real Rainbow assortment."

"Yeah," agreed Punk, "some one suggested 'Colours of Benetton' but we found out someone was already doing that. Some fashion brand or something."

"Well we can see the Indian right enough," said Russ, "but what about religion and the other bits."

"Easy mate," said D'Arcy, "we're Jewish, Moslem, Hindu, Christian and Buddhist. We're all here except for Buddha. He's contemplating his navel or something. He has to meditate to recharge his psyche, we just have a few extra beers."

"Well we reckon we can see who is the Hindu, but what about the rest of you?" asked Aussie Dad, "can't see much difference really."

"That's the point the world over 'ennit, no difference really?" said Punk.

"Oh boy! I tell you we are not going to show you our circumcisions," laughed David, "because we've all been done funnily enough so the Nazis would have had a fine old confused time with us."

"Those bastards were confused pretty well most of the time, same as all extremists," Isabel shot in smartly, "knowing their lack of mentality they'd have just shot you all anyway."

"Better than sawing your fucking head off on TV. Takes a real sick bastard to do that," exclaimed Cooper, "There's a big difference between reluctantly causing war casualties, however terrible, and deliberate gloating, public, barbaric sadism. No excuses for it. While such people live the population of the whole world is in danger."

"Yeah, bring it on," shouted Brad, his face aflame, "they invite us to go and get 'em, so let's do it. But really do it, smash 'em with everything we've got, no half hearted pussy footing around. Do 'em in proper then leave 'em to sort out the mess themselves. They invited it, they got it, so let them inherit it. Don't stay around to help 'em pick up the pieces by giving 'em millions of corrupt aid. Having to do it for themselves 'd keep 'em occupied for years. Of course they'd blame us but they do that all the time anyway."

He paused for breath.

"Oh my god, I've birthed a Republican," Mom gasped.

"Got a point though," said Lance, "I know that Brad's a bit extreme but while we're trying so hard to understand everyone and misunderstanding everything they're just getting on with the job of killing. No understanding there is there pal? They're trying so hard to be offended by us that they offend everyone and don't give a damn."

"Yeah," cried Brad, "the more we try to understand them the more they try to kill us."

"Huh!" exclaimed Isabel, "unless we pay them millions in dirty blackmail money. What has that got to do with God? Nothing, they're making the rules up as they go along, prostituting a beautiful religion that has millions of believers."

"Then why don't they do something about it then? Take their religion back instead of letting it be highjacked." asked Lance, "this is supposed to be the 21st century, the century of love, progress and enlightenment but it seems the more you involve the gods then the worse it gets. Some idiots confuse going backwards with going forwards."

"Oh my, I might get pissed off with a lot of things and people, disagree and dislike, but I don't want to kill them if they disagree with me. Well not always, just sometimes. Depends on who it is really. Ex husbands should really be done in. Acting like animals if you ask me," said Jeanette, "what do you think about all this guys?" she asked the Band.

"Well some wars have to be fought," said Punk, "I mean wars of freedom of speech, of religion and of race ya know. I reckon the difference between terrorists and freedom fighters is that the aims of the terrorists cannot remotely nor reasonably be fullfilled. That's what makes them terrorists."

"Wish the Palestinians were fighting an honourable war of freedom though. Could understand that," mused Isabel, "The United Nations made Israel and Palestine equally free, both independent and interdependent, and the Arabs went and blew it. They interfered and started a war to exterminate and obliterate Israel, a legally set up country, and it's people. They have the bloody nerve to accuse others of not following UN resolutions yet they've not followed one ever themselves. They lost and it's been a cock up and downhill ever since. How dare the Israelis object to being wiped off the face of the earth just to oblige some fanatics."

"We all need friendly neighbours but who needs one like the Imam of Jerusalem back then. He told the moslems to unite, sweep the Jews into the sea and kill them all. Didn't leave much room for negotiation did he? Real example of mutual tolerance and respect. Right neighbourly gesture," said Jeanette. "Thousands of Palestinians left the new Israel thinking the Arabs would win and they could come back to an empty land," said Isabel, "big, big mistake. The millions upon millions of Arabs lost, couldn't wipe out Israel, so occupied Palestine instead. They've been crying ever since."

"Ironically Israel later won it back from the Arabs and later still started to hand it over to the Palestinians but they were led by a guy named Arafat who ballsed it up and fought Israel again. Called it an Intifadah because it sounded more romantic and confusing. Interfuckup more like it. Absolute nutcases, some people," D'Arcy added solemnly.

"I love all the crap about only being able to use reasonable force. Not just in the Middle East, but all over," said Mom, "who's to judge when those who shout loudest about it weren't even there? Stupid! I mean use your common sense. Supposing you have an automatic pistol and are surrounded by twenty thugs armed with knives and clubs who want to rob and harm you. They threaten you. So what do you do? You don't say oh dear I have a gun, a superior weapon so I won't use it. You don't aim for their legs either do you unless you're completely mad? You shoot, and you shoot as many as possible in a place that's going to stop them killing you. If they run you still shoot to make sure they don't come back. Anything else is insanity. If the survivors complain then tell 'em they should have stayed at home and not caused the trouble in the first place."

"Trouble makers now make a big fuss about historical borders and countries and who made the decisions to set them up in certain places but ninety-nine point nine percent of all countries in the world were once made up with artificial borders," said Russ, "either by force or agreement. Seemed sensible at the time. Problems came later if people didn't try or manage to fit in."

The whole lot of them by now had flushed faces.

They weren't just starting to get warmed up they were beginning to get somewhat heated.

Shouts were coming from all over. Not just from the families.

What?

"No borders, yeah!"

"Peace and separate states for Palestine and Israel and the rest to mind their own fucking business!"

"A free Kurdistan for the Kurds!"

"Independent Kashmir!"

"Democracy for Africa!"

"Tell China to leave Taiwan alone, stay away from Mongolia and get the fuck out of Tibet."

"Viva the Dalai Lama and whoever he's born into next!"

"Freedom, cry freedom!"

"Tell 'em to free Nelson Mandela!"

"They did you prick!"

"Oh! Then we shall overcome!"

"I wanna sit at the front of the bus!"

"You can, dickhead, but you don't go by bus. You've got a VW!"

"Oh! awlright!"

"Waltzing Mathilda!"

"I love my billablong!"

"Show us your Billabong and I'll show you my didgeridoo!"

"Hey, hey hey, everyone. Time out please. This is getting out of hand. We'll soon be banging drums and doing a war dance," Russ shouted loudly, "we are supposed to be the enlightened ones not rabble rousers. Some good sentiments guys but could be better expressed. We all have to get along somehow."

"Yeah, look," said Punk, "we here are different races, religions and colours but we're all Australian. Australia takes us in and accommodates us. It would be wrong if we asked Australia to become us. We should become Australian. The trouble starts with those who want to bring their old country with them. If it was so great there then why leave? Adapt man, adapt."

"As for me," said D'Arcy, "we are Moslem, Jew and Christian, we've all been circumcised, we all believe in one God, none of us worship idols, except for AC/DC and INXS and the Rolling Stones of course and we are all descended from Abraham. So what's your problem?"

"Me, obviously," laughed Bollywood, "I haven't got any of that but I have gotta family culture that's a bit confusing. My parents tell me, son, you are now a man, old enough to work, to vote and go to war. You can have credit cards and a bank account. You can marry and have children but you are not old enough to pick your own girlfriends and never will be. Mummy and Daddy do that. Especially Mummy. And as for daughters, crazy man, just crazy. No one can touch your sister but you can gang rape any one else's sister. The police don't mind. Where do these people get off?"

"Sounds more like when do they get off rather than where," joked Brad.

"Love 'em to death of course," said Bollywood, "but let us breath, let us loose. They confuse looser with loser."

"Keep your own culture up to a point, don't just willy nilly adopt a new one, but don't force it on others or keep it where it don't fit," offered Mom.

"All right for you," said Bollywood, "you've been allowed to wear jeans for ever. I come from a place where men wear baggy pants, shabby long shirts, skirts or dresses. The women are beautiful though. Great clothes, colours you can't believe. Thank god for women"

"I say amen to that," smiled Brad, "but I can't understand that if God is so great why does he change all the gorgeous young girls into wives?"

They were all looking so pleased with themselves after what they regarded as an enlightened intelligent discussion that they chose to ignore Brad.

He didn't notice it. He was used to it.

He didn't regard himself as a loser. He was in a family that realised differences but where no one was a loser. To them that sort of talk was rubbish. Those who said that you were a loser if you didn't win, didn't come first and said second place was losing, were talking a load of old bollocks.

Isabel thought of all those who took part in sports or other activities not because they would win but merely because they could. Others had shocking disabilities, disadvantages and wounds that meant that they could never come first. They were all winners until some ignorant pratt told them they weren't. Thousands ran marathons, not to win prize money for their own benefit and fame, but to collect thousands for those who couldn't. They were all winners. The real losers were those who thought you had to win. Of course it was great to win but it was also great to do it at all.

Teamwork and competition should go hand in hand, not cancel each other out.

Isabel nodded to herself, "good thinking girl."

"Hey Noddy," Brad exclaimed, noticing her shaking her head, "what's going on inside that network of yours?"

"Oh, just thoughts," smiled Isabel, "good thoughts inspired by you."

"Wow!" Brad shouted, "hear that folks? I not only defy scientific definition but inspire good thoughts."

"Yep, all you need now mate is a girl who loves an inspirational alien," Cooper laughed, "then you're well away."

"They must be perceptive though," mused Brad, "'cos I'm deep you know."

"Huh!" grinned Jeanette, "Bro' you're so deep that they'd have to dig from pole to pole before they found anything."

"I'm that deep am I?" Brad said thoughtfully, "always knew it of course."

"How well did he do at school?" asked Russ, "he never fails to amaze."

"Got good grades," Mom asserted strongly, "graduated on time. He's okay that boy. Educated ya know."

"Hmm," Jeanette mumbled, "just goes to prove that we're all education obsessed instead of being intelligence focussed."

"Can't understand this fast track thing," said Isabel, "where a young wet behind the ears leapfrogs over others to the top and I don't mean just because his Daddy's the CEO."

"I reckon a year of experience at the sharp end is worth three years in college. Do both and you're in with a chance," said Russ, "even then you should start at the bottom."

"Start at the start you mean," chuckled Jeanette, "just imagine applauding a runner who wins after starting halfway round the track. He's not covered the whole course has he? Studied it but not actually done it. Doesn't know what it is to have to stay the distance and who can judge if he has what it takes. Even if he's trained well he's not been tested."

"You do realise that you've been saying 'he' the whole time, don't you?" said Lance with a protesting tone in his voice," what's with the 'he' bit? Are you being sexist?"

"Ah! maybe we should use the neuter version. Call everything and everyone 'it' instead of using a gender all the time," suggested Russ, "I mean 'it' shouldn't confuse anyone should 'it' as political correctness wants to de-describe everything and everyone anyway. No descriptions allowed in case 'it's' prejudicial."

"Yer, for instance - a white middle aged female dressed all in black mugged an old Chinese lady after dragging her into a dark alley on Winston Churchill Boulevard becomes - an indiscriminate dressed 'it' in 'it's' prime of life robbed another 'it' of irrelevant nationality who showed signs of youth deprivation in a colourless alley situated on a re-actionary named street," Lance said while laughing out loud, "really help the police that one wouldn't it?"

"Why can't we spell out the difference? I mean ordinary language was invented for easy, clear communication not to confuse and obscure," said Punk.

"Right on, We invented poetry to do that bit didn't we?" said d'Arcy, "why not have words to distinguish sex. Nature does it. Male and female clearly different. So why not sexist and sexiste, chauvinist and chauviniste, police officers and police officistes, detectives and detecdivas. Same with colour. Nature did it quite naturally so why do we find it so difficult. The eskimos apparently have dozens of words for white. Except for the fact they're obviously colour blind it just goes to show how descriptive we can be as a species. Surely we are capable of discriminating between things without prejudice."

"Yeah! got it," cried Brad, "don't call 'em transvestites any more. Call 'em transvest'its'. I don't mind neutering anyone as long as they don't neuter me."

"I wish we could mute you at times," laughed Jeanette.

"Have a remote control, zap him off you mean?" Isabel grinned, "one day folks, one day!"

"Hell on wheels people! They say there's safety in numbers but I can't see it here for me," Brad protested, "treble the family and treble the trouble is my experience."

"Okay, then let's talk about someone else," agreed Lance, "who shall we rubbish now?"

There was silence for a while. They thought they had covered almost everything but it needed a little thought in case anything had been missed.

The silence was broken with a very philosophical question by Cooper, "right then, who's for beers, who's for wine and who's for the fancies? My shout this time, yours next. Let's get 'em in."

There was complete agreement.

Homeward Bound

For the first time in weeks everyone was subdued. It was the last day.

Families from two countries, renowned for friendliness and openness, had to go their separate ways.

It was amazing that people who had an opinion on everything and could talk the hind leg off a donkey suddenly found themselves lost for words.

Mom had mixed feelings. She had made new friends and could take away happy memories but had to leave her daughter behind.

The rest were glad to be going home, albeit in different directions, but at the same time were sad to be parting.

They went together well. None were of the strong, silent type. They were all of the ferocious, noisy variety. They had too much enthusiasm and energy to hide behind a wall of silence. To them the sound of silence was deafening. Keeping quiet and staying still was an unknown. Perhaps that's what gave such vitality to the two countries.

To them people who kept quiet obviously had little to say. They didn't care if sometimes what they said made them look silly. It was better than saying nothing at all.

Of course not everyone shared that view.

Like a famous writer, some thought that it was better to say nothing and be thought a fool rather than say something that proved you were.

Wunderwear Woman didn't worry about that. She believed another author who thought that for evil to succeed it was only necessary for good people to say nothing.

For Wunderwear saying nothing was sacrilege.

She was never going to keep quiet. Quieter yes, but quiet never.

It takes all sorts.

They were sitting at the airport in the departure lounge. All the goodbyes had been said and all the tears had been shed. Well maybe not all the tears.

It was time for the 'Yanks to go back Home' and the Aussies to go back to work.

They were sitting unusually silent waiting for their flight to be called.

Then.

"Wonder how things are back 'ome," mused Isabel, "sort of lost touch haven't we?"

"Won't be no different will it?" said Mom, "still shooting people. NRA as dumb as ever. Rich getting richer, poor getting poorer, whatever the level of employment or the state of the New York Stock Exchange. And as for that Tea Party thing, well!"

"Yeah, Tea Party. What a lame name," asked Brad curiously, "I mean tea for crissakes. What's wrong with coffee? A Tea Party is about as pantyhose as a Coffee Morning. Who thought that one up?"

"Heh, heh, heh," chuckled Mom, "a Republican of course."

"Where did they get all that crap? Where did it come from then?" asked Brad, unusually interested.

"To do with History," Mom replied.

"Recent or ancient," asked Brad.

"Not old ancient but definitely not recent," said Mom.

"Stupid though really isn't it?" stated Isabel, "I mean just imagine the English having a Druid Party, the Scots being the Rob Roys or the French being Napoleons and the Germans having a Mongol Resistance Party."

"I thought they did, they called themselves Nazis," laughed Lance.

"Ha bloody ha!" said Isabel, "all right then imagine some Italians calling themselves the Roman Orgies."

"Yeah, awesome, I'd go for that," cried Brad, "sign me up."

"Nah, you'd need to be the President to get into that one," said Lance, joining in for the first time.

"Just my luck to be born a disinherited Prince," Brad said in a downhearted voice.

"Those who say that there's no such thing as luck are talking out of their butts," Mom said firmly, "luck starts the day you're born. Where, how and why starts right there. You can't take a look around to see if your parents own a palace or a mud hut and make a decision to stay or go back in the womb and ask god to try again. Not possible."

"Yep and you're nuts if you think you can influence it. You can use or refuse it when and if it comes but you can't make luck happen," said Lance,

"Correct," Isabel agreed, "otherwise it wouldn't be luck would it?"

"Some go mad to try and turn it their way though, don't they? said Mom, looking around as though there should be more of the family there. She was going to take some time to get used to Jeanette being thousands of miles away. "They think the stars, or where things are, or what they have and wear that matter. They actually believe it and pay fortunes for information that is meaningless. I mean if the stars do anything they are not going to be selective are they. How many millions are born in the same month under the same stars at the same time? So are they all going to be following the same advice on the same day with millions of others following another star and different advice. Advice by the way that the pundits churn out identically over a period of time. They only have limited options so they have to frequently repeat them.

One month it is romance time for about twenty million Pisces all rushing around hungrily looking at the opposite sex for the big moment and then the next month it is the turn of a different load of idiots to go charging around doing the same thing. It's like making up swings and roundabouts. Magic mushrooms and magic roundabouts. Can you imagine that all the Sagittarians would not do business on a certain day or in a precise month because it was inauspicious.

What they gonna do? Send in sick notes? Robots for the time period then come alive again afterwards. What a load of bullshit. For a start the world would run out of paper! People! Oi Yoi Yoi! They're already mental robots to start with."

"Why do people go on believing?" said Isabel, "it's nearly always wrong. By the law of averages it will be right for a few. That's all. They believe because they want to believe I s'pose."

"What I wanna know is what is with this word inauspicious," said Brad, "it sounds dirty to me. Sort of associate it with sacrifices, chanting and all that. A bit primitive ya know."

"Well that's because it is," said Lance, "auspicious means you're good to kill someone and inauspicious means they're good to kill you. Generals do it all the time."

"What!?"

"Yep, the leaders of the different armies consulted their gods. Today they're called advisors or experts, it's always been misnamed intelligence. They used to be called priests or whatever, shook some bones, and made their decisions. Of cause their gods always said they would win on a certain day or particular time but then the enemy gods would say the same," Isabel chuckled, "someone had to be wrong but they still believed anyway. They claimed they read god's words wrongly. Of course they did because it was all wrong and a load of bollocks in the first place. The only reason they went through all that crap was to dodge the responsibility of trusting their own judgement. Had to have somebody to blame if they lost."

"Others blame different things. Like born under a bad sign," said Mom, "can't understand it."

"I can," said Brad, "I mean, like bad signs. Imagine being born under a sign like - 'disabled only; no parking; pick up point only; or tow away zone' - bad karma man, but 'deliveries only' could be smart."

"I can imagine 'drop off' right now," laughed Isabel.

"But there are some who look actually for an auspicious time to be born," said Mom, "okay if you try to get pregnant so as to give birth at a certain time but not if you get pregnant and then have an abortion or a caesarian because the birthdate isn't quite auspicious. For crissakes, humans have to ignorantly interfere in everything. Jesus! the baby tells you when it's right, nature's been doing it forever. Who you gonna believe, nature or a fake fortune teller? It's a no brainer. Thought humans were given intelligence, obviously some were left out."

"Yeah," said Brad, "didn't one of us say that the world population has grown too far and too fast? Nature just ran out of brains, not enough to go round."

"Why not suggest brain pooling then, rather like car pooling you know," Mom proposed smiling.

"God help anyone who shared with Brad," said Isabel.

They all laughed.

Their flight was called. They stood up with sighs all round and went home.

the end

But as with any story the end of one is only the beginning of another.

The Hayes
Family wish
you all a
beautiful life.